"Would you like to get married?"

Brooke laughed, unable to believe her ears. Had *the* Matt Cutter just proposed? Stunned, she shook her head to clear the cobwebs. She started walking to her car. "Goodbye, Mr. Cutter."

"Wait!" He fell into step with her.

She felt a magnetic pull toward him, as if he were reeling her in. Her skin tightened with awareness and a raw need she didn't recognize.

She couldn't give the logical answer that had lodged in her throat. She could only stare up at him. She noted the stern set of his jaw, his generous lower lip that made her want to rise up on tiptoe and kiss him.

She got into her car. He closed the door and rested his hands along the base of the open window. Leaning down, he gave her a grin that made her stomach do somersaults.

"Think about it."

Dear Reader,

There's something for *everyone* in a Silhouette Romance, be it moms (or daughters!) or women who've found—or who still seek!—that special man in their lives. Just revel in this month's diverse offerings as we continue to celebrate Silhouette's 20th Anniversary.

It's last stop: STORKVILLE, USA, as Karen Rose Smith winds this adorable series to its dramatic conclusion. A virgin with amnesia finds shelter in the town sheriff's home, but will she find lasting love with *Her Honor-Bound Lawman*? *New York Times* bestselling author Kasey Michaels brings her delightful trilogy THE CHANDLERS REQUEST... to an end with the sparkling bachelor-auction story *Raffling Ryan*. *The Millionaire's Waitress Wife* becomes the latest of THE BRUBAKER BRIDES as Carolyn Zane's much-loved miniseries continues.

In the second installment of Donna Clayton's SINGLE DOCTOR DADS, *The Doctor's Medicine Woman* holds the key to his adoption of twin Native American boys—and to his guarded heart. *The Third Kiss* is a charmer from Leanna Wilson—a must-read pretend engagement story! And a one-night marriage that began with "The Wedding March" leads to *The Wedding Lullaby* in Melissa McClone's latest offering....

Next month, return to Romance for more of THE BRUBAKER BRIDES and SINGLE DOCTOR DADS, as well as the newest title in Sandra Steffen's BACHELOR GULCH series!

Happy Reading!

Mary-Theresa Hussey

Mary-Theresa Hussey
Senior Editor

Please address questions and book requests to:
Silhouette Reader Service
U.S.: 3010 Walden Ave., P.O. Box 1325, Buffalo, NY 14269
Canadian: P.O. Box 609, Fort Erie, Ont. L2A 5X3

The Third Kiss

LEANNA WILSON

SILHOUETTE *Romance*

Published by Silhouette Books

America's Publisher of Contemporary Romance

To
Grandpa Glenn,
a prince of a father-in-law

 SILHOUETTE BOOKS

ISBN 0-373-19484-6

THE THIRD KISS

This edition published by arrangement with Harlequin Books S.A.

® and TM are trademarks of Harlequin Books S.A., used under license.
Trademarks indicated with ® are registered in the United States Patent
and Trademark Office, the Canadian Trade Marks Office and in other
countries.

Visit Silhouette at www.eHarlequin.com

Printed in U.S.A.

Books by Leanna Wilson

Silhouette Romance

Strong, Silent Cowboy #1179
Christmas in July #1197
Lone Star Rancher #1231
His Tomboy Bride #1305
Are You My Daddy? #1331
Babies, Rattles and Cribs... Oh, My! #1378
The Double Heart Ranch #1430
The Third Kiss #1484

Silhouette Books

Fortunes of Texas
The Expectant Secretary

LEANNA WILSON

believes nothing is better than dreaming up characters and stories and having readers enjoy them as she does. Leanna is the winner of the National Readers' Choice Award and Romance Writers of America's Golden Heart Award. Married to her real-life hero, she lives outside Dallas with their active toddler and newborn. But all the diapers and lullabies haven't kept her from writing. She's busy working on her next book, be it a Silhouette Romance, Harlequin Temptation or Harlequin American Romance novel. She enjoys hearing from her readers, so you can write to her c/o: Leanna Wilson, P.O. Box 294227, Lewisville, TX 75029-4277.

IT'S OUR 20ᵗʰ ANNIVERSARY!
We'll be celebrating all year,
Continuing with these fabulous titles,
On sale in November 2000.

Desire

#1327 Marriage Prey
Annette Broadrick

#1328 Her Perfect Man
Mary Lynn Baxter

#1329 A Cowboy's Gift
Anne McAllister

#1330 Husband--or Enemy?
Caroline Cross

#1331 The Virgin and the Vengeful Groom
Dixie Browning

#1332 Night Wind's Woman
Sheri WhiteFeather

Romance

#1480 Her Honor-Bound Lawman
Karen Rose Smith

#1481 Raffling Ryan
Kasey Michaels

#1482 The Millionaire's Waitress Wife
Carolyn Zane

#1483 The Doctor's Medicine Woman
Donna Clayton

#1484 The Third Kiss
Leanna Wilson

#1485 The Wedding Lullaby
Melissa McClone

Special Edition

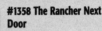

#1357 A Man Alone
Lindsay McKenna

#1358 The Rancher Next Door
Susan Mallery

#1359 Sophie's Scandal
Penny Richards

#1360 The Bridal Quest
Jennifer Mikels

#1361 Baby of Convenience
Diana Whitney

#1362 Just Eight Months Old...
Tori Carrington

Intimate Moments

#1039 The Brands Who Came for Christmas
Maggie Shayne

#1040 Hero at Large
Robyn Amos

#1041 Made for Each Other
Doreen Owens Malek

#1042 Hero for Hire
Marie Ferrarella

#1043 Dangerous Liaisons
Maggie Price

#1044 Dad in Blue
Shelley Cooper

Chapter One

"Do you ever think how much easier life would be if you could find Prince Charming?" Peggy mused, scuffing the sole of her boot on the sidewalk.

"No," Brooke Watson answered without hesitation. "But I could use a fairy godmother and a little of her magic." Not to look for a husband, but to find a miracle for one of her troubled young clients. Men, she'd decided many years ago, only complicated her life.

She'd seen too many dysfunctional marriages during her tenure as a child psychologist. Not to mention her own mother's penchant for collecting husbands the way her young clients collected and traded Pokémon cards.

"I could use some magic to pay off my credit card bills. Ohh, look! Another sale!" Peggy passed a streetlamp and steered Brooke toward Cutter's Western Wear.

It was the oldest department store in San Antonio,

situated along the winding, scenic River Walk. The Cutter family history went all the way back to the Alamo. They graced both the business and society sections of the paper weekly. At least the handsome heir and CEO did. What was his name? Brooke couldn't recall, nor did she want to remember. She had no use for spoiled rich men. She had better things to do with her time.

"Last stop," she said, following her friend through the door shaped like a chuck wagon's tailgate. "Then I need to get back home."

"And work?" Peggy complained.

It wasn't just work. She was committed to helping the children placed in her care.

A woman sped past her, knocking into her with a sharp elbow. Brooke shook her head with consternation. Must be some sale, Brooke thought to herself.

Peggy looked over her shoulder, "Maybe you can find some new jeans."

"What's wrong with mine?" Brooke asked, glancing down at her faded Wrangler jeans. Some of her patients didn't even have clothes to call their own. "Took me a few years just to break these in."

Brooke walked beneath a banner, and a storm of commotion erupted around her. Sirens wailed. A mariachi band kicked into high gear, the trumpets blaring, a drum's rhythm vibrating in her ears. A band? What the heck was happening?

Brooke faltered but kept moving forward with the surging crowd behind her. A chorus of cheers erupted from the customers packing into the store like sardines. Clapping thundered in her ears, echoing the beat of her heart. She glanced around and noticed vibrant red and yellow balloons clustered together. A wave of balloons tumbled over her with ribbons and tiny bits of paper twirling in the air conditioner's breeze. Bright crepe paper decorations were strung along the windows and across the ceiling. She blinked against the waterfall of confetti.

What was this, a party? A surprise party? Had the guest of honor arrived behind her? Must be someone famous. Maybe even the head of Cutter Enterprises.

Turning, Brooke searched the crowd but saw no one she recognized. But then, she didn't keep track of celebrities. Deciding it was time to go home, she searched for Peggy.

Her friend stood a few feet in front of her. She'd dropped her packages at her feet. Her features brightened with surprise and delight. "You did it. You're the one, Brooke!"

"Did what?" Had she set off some weird shoplifting alarm? She wasn't carrying any merchandise. Heck, she hadn't even made it to the rows of boots, Stetsons and jeans. "What'd I do?"

Like the Red Sea parting, the wall of people in front of Brooke opened up. A tall man, wearing a black Stetson that shaded his deep-set, midnight-blue eyes, stepped forward. Instantly she recognized the famous Cutter.

She'd seen his picture prominently displayed on television and in the papers ever since he'd taken over his family's company. He was the Cutter family's pride and CEO, San Antonio's Prince Charming, every woman's fantasy.

Every woman except her.

She had to admit he was even sexier and more virile in person than any of the photos she'd ever seen. An energy seemed to radiate off him like heat shimmers off asphalt. He drew everyone's attention, including Brooke's.

Then Brooke noticed that his penetrating, unnerving gaze was aimed at her. He moved toward her, gave her a knock-your-boots-off smile, doffed his cowboy hat, revealing thick, wavy black hair, and held out his hand. To her!

"Welcome to Cutter's." His voice sounded as deep and rich as his wealthy pockets. "I'm Matt Cutter."

Numbed by the shrill music and chaos, her brain clicked into autopilot. She shook his hand. But there was nothing mechanical or common about his warm palm pressed against hers, the strength in his fingers engulfing her hand or the electric shock that jarred her out of her trance.

Every nerve ending in her body vibrated. Her senses sharpened, blocking out the confusion and noise around her. Confident and bold, he took center stage, similar to the way he'd taken over his family's company a few years back. His gaze was as intense and focused as a spotlight.

Brooke's pulse skittered crazily in response. She noticed the way his Western shirt and jeans accented his broad shoulders, trim torso, slim hips and long, well-muscled legs. For an instant her brain registered that his starched jeans were slightly faded and the seam along his fly frayed. Awareness, red-hot and shocking, rocked through her.

Giving herself a mental shake, she blinked and withdrew her hand. Brooke cloaked herself in a professional demeanor, the one she used when a client shocked her with some intimate or appalling fact.

"Do you welcome all your customers with this

much fanfare?'' she asked, her voice lifting above the racket from the band and crowd.

His eyes brightened with humor, making them magnetic, and the corners crinkled. He grinned, throwing her off balance again. She had to get her reaction to him under control. What was wrong with her? Maybe the heat of the summer day had gotten to her. Or maybe it was the noise surrounding them, crowding her.

''Not usually,'' he said. His words were laced with laughter, making his voice rich, vibrant, irresistible. ''But we've made an exception. Just for you.''

The way his voice dropped, emphasizing the last word, made the statement intimate and caused her stomach to dip crazily. She could almost believe him, almost imagine him waiting for her. Just her.

You've lost it, Brooke. Really lost it!

She shook loose the strange effect he had on her and held her hand against her jumpy stomach. He was resistible. Just like every man she'd ever met. Prince Charming was a fairy tale, a feminine fantasy created to compensate for the helplessness women often felt. Well, she was *not* powerless.

Besides, Prince Charming had never worn a Stetson.

''You're our one millionth customer,'' he said, his eyes glittering as flashes of cameras went off around them like fireworks. ''Congratulations.''

''But I didn't buy anything.'' She protested, wishing her fairy godmother would suddenly appear, wave her magic wand and make her vanish into thin air. The sudden attention made her squirm inside. Or maybe the odd sensation was Matt Cutter's fault. No, she wouldn't accept that possibility.

"You didn't have to purchase anything. You're the millionth customer to visit our original store."

Her face burned with the same self-consciousness she'd experienced as a teen when her mother had forced her to attend all those debutante balls. She'd resisted, rebelled against the spectacle. She much preferred her quiet, uncomplicated life to this chaos.

The crowd seemed to be staring right at her. Or envying her, she thought, as she noticed women jostling each other to get a closer look at the CEO of Cutter Enterprises. She tried to ignore her own reaction to his charismatic eyes and chiseled features.

"But *customer,*" she argued, "implies I bought something. I didn't intend to—"

He closed the gap between them and cut off her remark. "You didn't have to."

His nearness frayed her carefully controlled nerves. "Why don't you pick someone else?"

Hands shot into the air, vying for Matt's attention. Brooke's ears rang as the women surrounding them called out to Matt, "Pick me! Me! Me!"

Matt shook his head. "You're the one."

"I don't want to be the one." His one. Anyone's one!

"Neither of us has a choice." His gaze sharpened, and she had a keen sense that he would have liked to have chosen someone else. Anyone else. She wasn't headline material. She wasn't the type of woman to grace covers of magazines. She was ordinary…plain. And difficult.

Peggy jostled her arm. "Your mother is going to flip!"

Brooke shuddered to think of her mother's reaction. "The only thing that would make my mother happy is if I showed up with a husband. You're not selling any of those, are you, Matt Cutter?''

"Maybe she'll be impressed with a few other prizes," Matt said, looping her arm through his. When he tucked her close to his side she felt as hot as a Texas heat wave.

Pressed against his well-honed frame, Brooke heard alarms go off in her head. He made her feel weak, fragile and incredibly feminine. She bucked against that assessment. But she couldn't move away from him, no matter how much she wanted to. He held her firmly against his side.

"Don't argue," he whispered, his voice compelling. He gave a smiling nod toward the cameras while moving her toward a platform and up the steps. "You're the winner."

But she didn't want to win. She didn't need anything. Not when so many others needed so much more. Faces of children she'd worked with through the years filed through her mind.

"Come on." He allowed no other arguments. He faced the audience and kept his hand on her arm as if she might bolt at any second. And she might have. If he'd given her the chance.

Irritation nettled her. She decided in that instant that Matt Cutter might be handsome, even sexy, but he was arrogant, domineering and overbearing.

"Good afternoon!" He spoke into a microphone, his voice resounding through the store and reverberating through her entire body. "Cutter's Western Wear is proud to announce we have now welcomed our one millionth customer."

Another cheer went up, and more flashes went off in front of Brooke's eyes, making her see spots.

"Tell us your name, Miss..." His focus, as well as the crowd's, shifted toward her.

She considered giving another name. Maybe even Peggy's. She couldn't imagine how this would look to her clients. Their psychologist making the headlines. But if nothing else she was honest, and so she spoke into the microphone. "Brooke," she said, "Brooke Watson."

"Well, Brooke," Matt Cutter said, slipping his arm around her waist, holding her close, making her skin tingle, "today is your lucky day."

Brooke wondered then if maybe she did have a fairy godmother, who'd gone overboard with the magic.

Matt Cutter had never met a more exasperating woman!

He admitted Brooke Watson had warm-brown eyes and a body that could make any red-blooded American male break out in a hormone-overloaded sweat. But what kind of woman resisted all he had to offer...er, all his store had to offer? He'd expected the millionth customer to gush, blush, maybe even throw herself at him. But he hadn't expected this woman's chilly reluctance and stubborn resistance.

He sure hadn't expected to be attracted to her, either.

"I really can't accept this," Brooke repeated, stepping back from the microphone and him.

He frowned. Maybe she hadn't understood. "It's a lifetime supply of jeans."

"I don't need any jeans. I like the ones I have."

He admitted her jeans looked sexy, the way they hugged her like an intimate embrace, caressing every feminine curve she had. His appreciative gaze swept over the tall, willowy brunette. "Those won't last forever."

She shrugged. "They'll last longer than some things."

What the hell did she mean by that?

"Look," she offered, "if you *have* to give away a lifetime supply of jeans, then I'll choose who they go to."

She scanned the crowd. Everyone went berserk, screaming and hollering, waving and jumping, trying to get Brooke's attention. Then she smiled, really smiled, for the first time since he'd met her. And it gave his stomach a strange sensation.

"The lifetime supply of jeans goes to—" she grinned while he gritted his teeth "—this woman in front. Peggy Simmons."

The redhead raised her arms like Rocky, after winning the championship fight, and turned in a tight circle.

Now what was he going to do? Brooke gave away prizes as if she was cleaning out her closet of the past year's clothes. What was wrong with her? What woman didn't want clothes? Maybe she simply didn't wear jeans often enough to justify a lifetime supply. Fine. But she wouldn't be able to resist the next prize.

"That was very generous of you," he said into the mike, well aware of the cameras aimed at him and of the wall of reporters taping every word. Maybe the circus atmosphere Brooke had generated would create bigger headlines. Definitely a plus for Cutter's. "Now, for this next gift you'll have to sit here."

"But I don't—"

"Sit." He barked the command as if to his black

Lab, Dodger, and jerked the microphone behind his back.

Brooke snapped her mouth closed and glared at him.

Maybe that wasn't the right approach for this woman. He touched her arm gently, even though he wanted to grab her. This woman brought out a Neanderthal side of him. "Look, it won't take long. I won't hurt you," he said softly so only she could hear. "Promise."

"I'm not afraid of you."

He ground his teeth and edged closer to her, challenging her, daring her not to step back toward the chair. In spite of her height, she still didn't meet his chin and had to crane her neck to glower at him. "That's right, Miss Watson. Right over there."

"Doctor. It's Dr. Watson," she corrected him in a clipped tone that set his nerves on edge.

A doctor, eh? He could see that. He could see a lot of things in this woman, some of which he didn't particularly like. But he saw many things he did appreciate, like the deep-rose of her lips, the way the tip of her nose tilted up, the challenge in her toffee-colored eyes. He especially liked the way she didn't back down. She stood her ground, never retreating, like so many women he'd known who would have bent over backward to please him. Maybe that's what attracted him. But that was absurd! Because this spitfire of a woman annoyed the hell out of him.

She stood toe-to-toe with him. Actually, her breasts brushed against his chest and tied his insides into knots. Trying to ignore the way she affected him, he pushed on. She gave an inch, then another. They inched their way across the platform until she backed into the chair and plopped into the seat with a thud.

"Perfect." He took a deeper breath, now that he couldn't feel her against him or imagine what she'd be like wrapped within his embrace. But he couldn't let her escape. Not until he'd finished with her. Finished giving her all she deserved. All the presents for being the millionth customer, that is. Keeping his hand on her arm, he glanced over his shoulder for his assistant to bring the next gift.

"This is a coveted prize, Dr. Watson," he said, giving her a subtle warning that he wouldn't tolerate her giving this one away. Lifting the mike, he announced, "The next prize for our valued millionth customer is a pair of custom boots made exclusively here at Cutter's!"

A satisfactory ah-h-h went through the crowd. Feeling confident, he knelt beside her chair, gave her a wink and pulled Brooke's tennis shoe off. He tossed it over his shoulder, and it landed with a dull thud on the platform.

"Hey! Give me back my shoe." She reached for it, and he grabbed her hand.

It was a battle of wills that he hadn't played with a woman in a long time. If ever. And he was determined to win.

"I'm going to give you something better than that old tennis shoe." He placed the mike on the floor behind him so their voices wouldn't carry. Then he trapped her foot against his thigh.

Her eyes widened. His insides burned. A staggering heat seemed to fuse them together. Or maybe it was his imagination. Maybe it was the flashes from the cameras. Maybe the crowd was pressing too close.

Touching Brooke was definitely a mistake.

Her toes curled in protest and made his skin tighten with need. Blood pumped hot and fierce through him. What was she doing to him?

"I like my tennis shoe," she said through gritted teeth. "Let go of my foot."

"I'm only going to measure it."

"Measure someone else's. Let me choose another—"

"No." His temper snapped.

Why couldn't someone else have been the millionth customer? She tried to pull her foot away, but he held firm. Until she winced. Guilt shot through him. Quickly he closed both hands over her foot and soothed the place he'd injured. He kneaded her instep. Beneath the thick sports sock, he felt her fine bones, her warmth. Slowly she relaxed. The center of her eyes dilated with awareness. *Keep your hands to yourself, Cutter!*

"I'm sorry." He forced himself to quit massaging her foot and get through with this procedure. "Now be still. This will only take a minute."

Her shoulders stiffened at his instructions. He slid the foot-measuring plate between her foot and his thigh. The cold metal chilled his overactive libido.

"A perfect six," he said, "but very narrow." Then he measured the length from her ankle to her knee, sliding the measuring tape along the curve of her calf. He felt her tremble. She tried to pull away from him, but he held firm. "Your boots will be ready in six weeks, Miss...Doctor. What color would you like? White to go with your doctor coat?"

"I'm not that kind of doc."

He raised an eyebrow. "A professor then?"

"A psychologist."

Definite trouble. "How about black for troubled souls?"

"Or for your black eye if you don't let go of my foot."

She was one feisty filly. He laughed, taking more pleasure in the anger sparking in her eyes. Abruptly he released her foot and stood.

Though he dreaded bringing out the grand prize, he had no choice. Everything had all been staged, and it was too late to turn the tide. Seeing it move toward them like a float in the Rose Parade, he reached for the microphone.

"Now, ladies and gentleman and doctors, too." His eyes darted toward Brooke. She was reaching for her wayward tennis shoe. "Here's the grand prize." Matt reached into his pocket for the keys. "Your very own convertible!"

The crowd went wild as the tiny roadster was wheeled to the front of the platform. Brooke dropped her shoe, her mouth gaping before she recovered, her gaze slicing toward Matt for confirmation.

"You don't want that!" someone yelled. "Give it to me!"

"How 'bout me, honey?" a man from the back hollered. "I could sure use a date magnet like that."

Matt's eyes narrowed with irritation. He took Brooke's hand and closed her fingers around the keys. "The car is yours. Understand?"

She locked gazes with him. He felt an electric shock right in the middle of his chest, as if she'd zapped him with a cattle prod.

"Could I have a van instead?" she asked.

Her question stunned him. Now, after all this time, she was going to get greedy? "What?"

"A van. You know with sliding doors on both sides."

He knew he would regret asking, but he couldn't stop himself, "Why?"

This time, she leaned toward the microphone. "I'm going to donate this car...well, van...to an orphanage here in town."

The crowd fell silent. It felt as if the air had been sucked out of the room and every greedy hand waver chastised.

"An orphanage?" Matt repeated.

She nodded. "They really need a vehicle to transport the children for doctor appointments and special events. So if you don't mind...?"

She pushed the keys back toward him, putting the ball in his court. How could he say no?

Slowly light applause trickled through the crowd, and Matt's attitude toward Brooke suddenly changed. An orphanage. How many people would do something like that? Not many. He gave her a nod of approval.

"Cutter's would be glad to trade this car in for a vehicle that will help the orphanage."

Finally Brooke gave him a smile that melted the cynicism surrounding his heart. This woman amazed, confounded and confused him. And that spelled trouble.

"What else do I get?" Brooke asked. Luckily her voice didn't carry to the mike.

What else? Maybe he'd been wrong about her. Maybe he'd wanted to believe there was someone out there who wasn't interested in money or what he could give them.

"What more do you want?" he asked.

"Isn't there a sign over in the window saying something about a million pennies?"

He'd forgotten. This woman distracted him, jumbled his thoughts, discombobulated him. "Are you going to keep this one?"

She lifted her chin with a challenge. "Why don't you find out?"

Chapter Two

Enough celebration for one day.

Enough Brooke Watson...or Dr. Brooke Watson...forever.

Matt strode down the hospital corridor, intent on forgetting his irritation over the millionth customer debacle. More important things concerned him.

The antiseptic smells made him scowl as he made his way past the nurses' station. But Brooke's clean, fresh scent of soap and sunshine lingered with him, permeated his thoughts and kept him thinking of her long, sexy, jeans-clad legs.

What was the matter with him?

Tempering his scowl, he opened the door to room 517 and gave a warm smile to the fragile woman in the hospital bed. "Hello, darlin'."

Her gaze shifted from the television set to Matt. He saw the spark return to her vibrant blue eyes, and her weathered face creased with a faint smile. "How did it go?'' She held out her hand, beckoning him closer. ''I want to hear all about it.''

''In time,'' he said, settling himself on the edge of the bed, mindful of the IV tubes. He took her frail hand in his and kissed it. ''How are you today, Grandmother? Feeling any better?''

''Feel just like a pin cushion.''

''More needles, eh?''

''Useless waste of time. There's not a damn thing they can do for old age. Comes a time when a body's ready to give out.''

Every one of his muscles tensed, and his heart contracted with fear and worry. ''Don't talk that way, Grandmother. You're as young as—''

''An old goat. Don't fool yourself, Matt, darling. My time's coming. I'm at peace with it.'' She patted his hand as if to soothe him, when it should have been the other way around. ''I'm just sad I won't live long enough to see you married and happy.''

She said it as if marriage was synonymous with a cheerful state of mind. Which didn't compute with him.

''Well, I'm happy,'' he said, trying to keep the conversation light. ''Happily single. One out of two isn't bad.''

The wrinkled skin between her faded brows pinched tight.

''Don't you worry. Soon as you're feeling better you'll have plenty of time to set me up with more of your friends' nieces and granddaughters.'' She'd been playing matchmaker for years now, and Matt had taken it in stride but at the same time had easily sidestepped matrimony. ''I might even surprise everyone and get married one of these days.''

"You tease."

His grandmother was right. He wasn't looking for a wife. He didn't have anything against marriage. He simply wanted to be sure a woman wanted him. Not his fortune. Which seemed impossible, especially with the women he'd dated, who were as money hungry as tigers on the prowl.

Eliza Louise Cutter gave his hand a squeeze. "You're not happy, Matt. Believe me, if you were to find true love, the way your grandfather and I loved each other, then you'd understand why it's so important. It will make and keep you young at heart. That's one reason I'm not afraid to leave this life. At least I'll be with your grandfather again. My dear, sweet Linc."

"Don't talk that way…"

She tsked him. "Go ahead and tell me how the big celebration went."

He gave a frustrated sigh and wished he could convince her that she had years and years left. It was as if she'd given up! As if she wanted to die. "It was more like an auction. She—"

"She?"

"The millionth customer. An exasperating woman if I ever met one. She was giving away all the prizes."

"Giving them away?"

He nodded gravely. "She gave the lifetime supply of jeans to a friend. And she asked for the roadster to be traded for a van so she could give it to an orphanage. Can you believe that?"

"Sounds like a levelheaded woman. And a generous one." His grandmother gave an approving nod. She carefully folded back a portion of the white hospital sheet. "Exasperating, huh? I do believe that's what Linc said about me when we first met. I told you about that, didn't I?"

"Once or twice." He grinned.

She waved her hand, dismissing her fond memories. "You just don't like changes. Never have. But maybe it worked out for the best. Maybe this exasperating woman's generosity will stir up more publicity for the store. And more important, maybe it did a little good for the community."

If anyone knew the meaning of generosity, he did. He'd learned it from his grandparents. Where his parents had been selfish, using their millions for indulgences and self-gratifying motives, Eliza and Linc Cutter had given not only gobs of money but gold bullions of time. Matt had been a recipient in more ways than one.

So why had Brooke Watson's altruism irritated him? He simply didn't like it when his plans veered off course.

He decided to play the devil's advocate. "It could look as if this woman didn't like our products. As if our merchandise wasn't good enough for her."

His argument lacked conviction. He hated to admit he'd been impressed with her. Too impressed. Too aroused. Especially when they'd stood toe-to-toe. He didn't want to think how close he'd come to grabbing her and kissing her. What a headline that would have been!

"What did she do with the million pennies?" Eliza asked.

"Hmm?"

"That exasperating woman," she quoted him, her

mouth lifting in a smile. "What did she do with the million pennies?"

He shook loose his raging hormones. "She gave them to a local school."

He'd anticipated her wanting the money for herself, or maybe even asking for more. But she hadn't. She'd simply promised the money to a bunch of needy kids.

His previous annoyance had grudgingly changed to approval. Why had he wanted to dislike Brooke Watson so much? He shrugged off that question, refusing to touch it as if it were the electric fence surrounding Fort Knox.

"She seems thoughtful and caring," his grandmother mused. "Sounds like a nice woman. Not exasperating at all."

How about irritating, infuriating, maddening? He pictured Brooke. None of those words came to mind. Only *beautiful, sexy, tempting*. Trouble, he decided.

"What did she look like?"

"Hmm?" Her question jarred him from his thoughts.

A twinkle sparkled in his grandmother's eye. He wished he could keep that sparkle there and make her want to continue living. "What did she look like?"

"I can't really remember, Grandmother." Actually he couldn't forget.

Eliza's papery brow wrinkled into a frown.

Immediately he felt a jolt of concern to his heart. "What's wrong? Are you feeling bad? Do you need a nurse?"

"No, no, darling. I'm fine. As fine as I can be, confined to this bed. I'm just wishing you could find a woman...someone kind and generous...like that woman who won. But someone who would light your fire.'' She waggled her silvery-gray eyebrows.

''Grandmother!''

She chuckled softly, then leaned her head back against the pillow and closed her eyes. Faint blue veins made a delicate pattern across her eyelids. ''Someday you'll find her. I just wish I could live long enough to meet the woman who's going to knock your socks off.''

''Don't worry yourself sick.'' He placed a kiss on her cheek. ''I'll be back tomorrow. Call if you need anything before then.''

She nodded but didn't open her eyes. Reluctant to leave, he hovered near the doorway until her breathing fell into the rhythm of sleep. A constriction cut off his own oxygen supply. She was all he had. All he'd ever had. She'd raised him, loved him when his parents had been too busy trekking around the world, spending money as if it was grown on trees and forgetting they had a family business to run and a son to raise. So his grandmother had stepped in to care for him. Now he'd do anything…*anything*… for her.

Anything, huh?

Would he be willing to make her last wish come true? With that simple question, an outrageous plan locked into place. Why not? Why couldn't he do this one thing for her, when she'd sacrificed so much for him? She'd taken time away from her beloved Linc to raise him, going to all his baseball games, tennis matches and golf tournaments. Why couldn't he make this one sacrifice for her? After all, it wouldn't have to be forever. Only until…

He winced at that thought. He couldn't think of her

dying. But he could concentrate on making his grandmother the happiest woman alive. If that was her last
wish, then, by God, he'd see that she had it. He'd find
himself a bride. A temporary bride.

But who?

His mind clicked into gear, keeping pace with each
clunk of his boot heels against the linoleum floor as
he strode back down the hallway toward the elevator.
It didn't take long for him to land on a possibility.
His *only* possibility.

*The only thing that would make my mother happy
is if I showed up with a husband.* Brooke Watson's
words came back to him full force.

Of course. She's the one!

She had incentive. Just as he did.

But she hadn't lunged for his wallet. So maybe
she'd be willing to give him his ring back after a
short, fake engagement, the way she'd given away all
his prizes.

He congratulated himself on a fine plan. This
would be a piece of cake. A piece of wedding cake!

"Why don't we read this book together, Jeffrey?"
Brooke kept her voice upbeat even when she felt de-
feated once more by this reticent five-year-old.

He kept his head bent, never looking up, never re-
sponding. A shock of brown hair fell across his forehead, and she smoothed it back. At least he no longer
flinched.

"This is one of my favorites. Have you ever read
it?" She continued talking, though she felt as if she
was talking to a brick wall.

But she didn't stop. She plowed ahead, opening the
book, showing him the pages. If he would only look

up enough to see the bright, colorful carnival pictures of cotton candy, popcorn and clowns. She'd just reached the second page when a shadow crossed the book. With a sigh she stopped. Was it already time for her to leave?

Expecting to see the prim and stoic Mrs. Morris who ran the orphanage, she glanced up and felt the breath knock out of her lungs. "What do you want?"

Matt Cutter gave her that charming grin she was sure had made many women swoon. But not her. He didn't faze her in the least. Not even those navy-blue eyes that seemed deeper than the ocean and as full of as many mysteries. She refused to notice the way his starched white shirt emphasized his tan or the way his faded jeans fit a tad too snugly, causing a heat flash inside her.

"I came to see you." His deep, sexy voice made the back of her neck tingle.

She closed the book. What did he want now? She'd taken enough grief from friends and co-workers the past couple of days to keep her permanently out of the limelight. It was all Matt's fault. Men like him were trouble. Pure and simple. "How'd you find me?"

"It's not a secret that you come here every Monday, Wednesday and Friday, is it?"

"No, but—"

"Good, then your secretary isn't in trouble." He swiveled a kid-size chair toward him on its legs and settled into it as if it were as comfortable as a leather recliner. He stretched out his long legs and crossed them at the ankles, the toes of his custom black boots pointing toward the ceiling.

Irritation sparked inside her. How would he like

someone barging into one of his high-powered business meetings? "I'm in the middle of a session."

"Hey, cowboy," Matt addressed Jeffrey. "How are you?"

Her attention snapped toward the little boy who stared at Matt like he was Paul Bunyan reincarnated.

But he wasn't. He was a wealthy business owner. He'd franchised his family's store, taken it nationwide, diversified Cutter's assets and branched out beyond Stetsons and Ropers to retail clothes, fast food and oil. He bought and sold companies like most people borrowed books from the library. His rate of return with women was, according to the tabloids, even faster.

And here he was at a little, out-of-the-way orphanage, concentrating on a five-year-old as if he was about to make a business deal. "Do you mind my interrupting you and Dr. Watson for a minute?"

Brooke caught a small, almost indiscernible, shake of the little boy's head. But it was there! She wouldn't have believed it if she hadn't witnessed it. Her heartbeat kicked up its pace.

Unbelievable! She'd been working with Jeffrey for over six months and there had been only minuscule improvements. Most of her colleagues would have given up by now. Then Matt Cutter waltzes in the room and the kid merely acts shy, instead of traumatized. What was it about the famous cowboy? Who was he… Prince Charming in a Stetson?

That was dangerous thinking, even if she didn't want a Prince Charming. And she didn't.

Women acted as if he was Tom Cruise or something, swarming around him, fawning over him, buying up any newspapers, magazines or tabloids that printed his picture. Well, she didn't get it. Maybe that's why she was more irritated than delighted at Jeffrey's tiny response.

"What are y'all reading?" Matt asked, disturbing her thoughts even more as he turned the book over on her lap and brushed his hand against her thigh. A jolt of electricity coursed through her. "Hmm. Looks interesting. But carnivals and circuses are for little kids. Not big boys like you."

Annoyance nettled inside her, especially when she saw Jeffrey's eyes widen.

"I've got a book at home, cowboy, that I bet you'd like. It's about cowboys and horses. Would you like me to bring it sometime for you to read?"

Again, the little boy gave a microscopic indication that he would.

Amazed, Brooke wondered what magic Matt had woven in the few moments he'd been here. She stared at him, bewildered and confounded, but also impressed and baffled. This showed progress. And gave her hope for the little boy. But how had Matt accomplished so much in so little time?

Catching sight of Mrs. Morris walking the periphery of the rec room, wearing her brightly colored quilted vest, Brooke leaned toward the little boy. "Jeffrey, it's time for me to go, but I'll be back in a couple of days. Okay?"

No response. Frustration returned full force.

Trying to remain positive, she touched his shoulder lightly. "I'll bring you a cowboy book then, if you want."

She stood, indicating it was time for Matt to follow her. Picking up her briefcase and taking her childhood book away from Matt, she told Jeffrey goodbye and

turned on her heel. Mindful that the CEO was following at his own leisurely pace, she wondered if he was
surveying the orphanage, planning to buy it and turn
it into condos or a golf course. Men like Matt Cutter
always had their own agendas.

When she glanced over her shoulder to give a final
wave to Jeffrey, she almost tripped over her own two
feet. Matt Cutter was following her, all right—and
staring right at her behind! Instead of outrage she felt
a shiver of satisfaction ripple down her spine. Matt
Cutter dated only the most beautiful women—actresses and models, the crème de la crème.

Although she felt a boost to her womanly pride to
know he was looking at her with obvious desire,
that's where it ended. Because she did not want Matt
or his interest. No way. No how.

"Goodbye, Dr. Watson," Mrs. Morris said as
Brooke signed out for the day. "We'll see you
Wednesday."

"Yes, yes, fine." Straightening her thoughts as she
would a stack of wrinkled, ruffled papers, she sharpened her focus. "If there are any changes with Jeffrey…if you need me for anything…just call."

"Of course." The woman shifted her gaze and patted her graying pageboy cut. "And, goodbye, Mr.
Cutter. Come back anytime to visit. Anytime."

He stopped and gave the older woman's hand more
of a caress than a shake. Brooke tried not to roll her
eyes. Then he gave a nod to the receptionist and
flashed one of his famous smiles to the other gawking
workers lurking around doorways as if they had nothing better to do than stare at the famous CEO.

"It was a pleasure, ladies," he said with a wave.

A pleasure? Good grief! Was he running for public

office? She shoved her way out the door and into the glaring sunshine.

After reaching the curb, they walked through the parking lot. When she was sure they were out of hearing range of the orphanage, she turned on Matt Cutter with professional outrage. "What do you think you're doing? I was in the middle of a session and you barged in—"

"Whoa." Matt held up one hand in self-defense. "Mrs. Morris said your time was up, anyway. She was on her way over to take Jeffrey back to class. I simply interrupted for her."

He gave her his know-it-all grin that had zero effect on her. Except to aggravate her even more.

"A nice lady, Mrs. Morris," he said, apparently oblivious to Brooke's anger, or perhaps he was ignoring it. "She was gracious enough to show me where you were. Said it wouldn't hurt since Jeffrey doesn't respond to anyone." A frown pinched his forehead. "What's wrong with him, anyway?"

"It's unethical for me to discuss a patient. Besides, it's none of your business." She crossed her arms over her chest. The Texas sun beat down on her, causing a trickle of perspiration to slide down her spine. Or was Matt to blame for her sudden flush? "Now if you're here about those damn boots—"

"Easy, Cinderella. I didn't come bearing gifts, glass slippers or boots. But if that's what would make you smile, then I'll try to find something." He patted his shirt and pants pockets. "Or better yet, next time I'll bring a dozen roses with me."

She didn't want roses or anything else from this man. "Just get to your point. There is a point to your being here, isn't there?"

"Always."

She waited.

He watched her. Not really watched, but eyed her, sized her up, letting his gaze roam over her freely, intimately. She felt a shiver ripple through her that wasn't revulsion. It was awareness…arousal… alarming!

Why wasn't she insulted? Why didn't she want to slap his face? What made her suddenly think about kissing his arrogant mouth? She had to get away from this man. The faster the better.

"Well…" She tapped her toe.

His blue eyes glimmered with a low-burning heat that made her insides shift eagerly, no, restlessly. Uncomfortably, she corrected.

"Mind if we go somewhere where we can speak privately?" he asked.

"Yes, I do mind. I mind your intrusion in my schedule today. I mind standing in the heat, waiting for you to tell me what you want. I mind—"

"I offered to take you somewhere more comfortable—"

"Like your home?" she asked, knowing that would be like the spider inviting the fly into his web.

He edged toward her, his mouth pulling to one side in a tempting smile that unraveled her composure. "Is that what you would like?"

She jerked her chin. "I don't have time to stand around discussing the weather or anything else. Now either say what it is you came to say or you'll have to excuse me." To emphasize her point she checked her watch. "I have another appointment."

"Believe me, I didn't come here to discuss the weather." His heated gaze told her exactly what he was thinking about. It wasn't storm fronts or the local heat wave. But it did make her hot and bothered.

"What then, Mr. Cutter?"

"Matt."

Her mouth pinched at the corners. She didn't need to think of him as Matt or in any other personal way. "Mr. Cutter, you're going to make me late."

"Of course." He hooked his thumbs in his belt loops, making her gaze drop to the faded line of his zipper. She had lost her mind! Then he rocked back on his heels. "I apologize for any inconvenience in your schedule. If you want I could call and—"

"I don't want you to call. Now, please..."

He gave a sharp nod, making the brim of his Stetson dip, then rise. "I'll cut to the chase. How would you like to get married?"

She felt as though a bucket of ice-cold water had been tossed at her. "What?"

"Well, not really married. Engaged. Temporarily."

Her jaw dropped, and she snapped her mouth closed. "Are you nuts?"

"Probably."

Stunned, she gave a shake of her head to clear the cobwebs from her brain. Maybe she'd heard him wrong. But she didn't think so. "I don't have time for this nonsense." She started walking to her car. "Goodbye, Mr. Cutter."

"Wait!" He fell into step with her. "Hear me out."

"I don't think so."

"It's for a good cause."

She laughed, unable to believe the strange turn of events or even her own hearing. Had Matt Cutter, *the* Matt Cutter, just proposed to her? In an offhanded, casual way? "I'll bet. Your cause, right, Mr. Cutter? Or were you planning on donating a million to the orphanage here?"

"If that's what will make you agree, then I'll arrange it."

She stumbled to a stop. "You're serious?"

"As a stock market crash." He flicked the brim of his hat with his forefinger.

She felt a magnetic pull toward him, as if he were slowly reeling her in, closer, closer, closer… Until he could take a bite…or nip…or nuzzle. Her skin tightened with awareness and a raw need that she had rarely, if ever, felt. What would Peggy or her mother say if they'd heard Matt's proposal? *Grab him and never let go!*

What was happening here? It felt like a fairy tale or a dream or some wild fantasy. But it wasn't hers. Maybe her mother's. Or Peggy's.

But she couldn't seem to back away from Matt. She couldn't give the logical answer that had lodged in her throat. She could only stare up at him, feeling awestruck, dumbfounded, baffled.

She noted the serious look in his eyes, the stern set of his jaw, his generous lower lip that made her want to rise up on tiptoe and kiss him. The heat must have addled her brain.

"You're going to be late for your appointment, Doc."

She blinked and shook herself. "Uh, yeah…yes." She realized then that she'd reached her no-nonsense gray Ford. She fumbled with the keys, then remembered she'd left the windows down to alleviate the stifling heat. Opening the door, she slid into the sticky, hot seat. "But—"

He closed the door and rested his hands along the base of the open window. Leaning down, he gave her a grin that made her stomach turn completely over. ''Think about it. I'll be in touch.''

Chapter Three

I'll be in touch. That's all Brooke seemed capable of contemplating the rest of the day. Specifically, Matt's touch. And he hadn't even touched her!

Oh, yes, he had. When they'd first met. She could still feel the way her stomach had curled into a ball of longing when he'd caressed her foot. He hadn't caressed it, she argued to herself. He'd simply measured it.

Yeah, right!

"Did you decide?" Felicia Watson Holbrook Roberts Evans, minus or plus a few other surnames, sipped her white wine.

Jarred out of her musings, Brooke stared at her mother. Decide what? To marry Matt Cutter? It was absurd! Ludicrous! She couldn't even believe she was dwelling on his proposal. Obviously he had some warped agenda. Or had lost his mind. Maybe he needed therapy instead of a bride. She'd never met a man who didn't need psychotherapy. Either way, she was staying clear of him.

"Brooke?"

"Hmm?"

"Dinner." Felicia tapped her pale-pink, manicured nails on the leather bound menu. "Did you decide what you're having?"

How about Matt Cutter? Good grief! Her mother's and Peggy's attitudes had finally worn off on her.

"You've been reading that menu for what seems like hours."

She hadn't read one appetizer or even peered at the desserts. "What are you having, Mother?"

"The halibut."

"Sounds fine to me." Especially since she wasn't hungry.

After they'd ordered, Felicia clasped her hands and gave her daughter one of *those* looks. "What are you doing this Friday?"

She asked the question in a casual manner that Brooke knew was never offhanded. There was always purpose behind every word or deed.

Felicia had obviously decided to get down to business. Her business. Her agenda. Just as Brooke had known she would. It was always just a matter of time before her mother launched into her latest matchmaking scheme.

"Working probably." She let her gaze drift around the posh restaurant, noticing the glittering diamonds and understated but elegant clothes of the patrons. It made her think of the children at the orphanage, and she wondered what they were having for dinner tonight. Monday night—frankfurters and beans, cherry

Jell-O and chips. "I've got a stack of files that need updating."

A small frown creased the bridge between her mother's carefully plucked, brushed and styled eyebrows. It had taken thousands of dollars from ex-husband number four to remove any and all wrinkles daring to appear on her mother's face. But Felicia had never been one to worry about money. With each husband, she'd moved up the social ladder. Her latest acquisition was worth millions, which translated into a huge mansion, a Mercedes and all the diamonds and jewels her mother could want. Face-lifts, too.

"You'll simply have to put it off."

Here we go! "Who is it this time, Mother?"

"A charming man I met at a little lingerie boutique."

"Which one?" Brooke asked.

"What difference does it make?"

"If he was shopping for lingerie, then it probably means he's got a main squeeze."

"Brooke!"

She sipped her water and wished she'd ordered something stronger. This could be a long evening. "Mother, I've told you, I'm not in the market. I'm not interested in finding a man."

"Nonsense. You really should meet this one. He's just darling. Such a gentleman. Walked me to my car, carried my packages for me. What a dear!"

Brooke refrained from making a diagnosis and focused on buttering her roll. She'd made the mistake once, and only once, of actually meeting one of her mother's prime candidates. For years after that Felicia had thrown that disastrous date into her face, saying,

"If only you'd given Sterling a chance…"

"Well, of course, I understand why you're not interested." Her mother touched her left earlobe as if to check and make sure her three-carat diamond earring hadn't been lost or stolen. "Not after the weekend you had!"

Alarm bells sounded in Brooke's head. Damn. She knew.

"I can't believe you didn't call me the second you got home to tell me all about it. I had to hear it from Lisbeth Mabry. She saw it on the ten-o'clock news. Of course, I said it couldn't be *my* daughter. What would you be doing shopping at a retail shop? But she was adamant.

"Then I understood perfectly what you were doing there. You weren't shopping for boots or jeans. You were shopping for a man!" Her mother gave a victorious grin. "Finally!"

Her mother took a celebratory sip of wine. "Matt Cutter. Now, he's a catch. Wait till the women at the country club hear that my daughter has caught the richest man in Texas. They'll be perfectly ill with jealousy."

Brooke's temples began pounding.

"Now," her mother continued, "it makes sense why you wouldn't want to go out with some man your mother has found for you when you've got one of your own." She leaned forward, breaking one of her cardinal rules by resting her forearm on the edge of the table. Her azure-blue contacts glittered with excitement. "So tell me all about this Matt Cutter."

"What makes you think I have him? Er, could

have?'' Or want him? She didn't, of course.

"You could have any man you wanted. If you put your mind to it.''

"You mean, if I set a trap for him.''

"A trap.'' She tsked. "Having your hair and nails done is not a trap. It's garnish. Simply shows a man you're willing to go the extra mile to please him. Clothes are simply an accessory to lure them in, make them appreciate what's—'' she lowered her voice to a whisper "—underneath.''

"You know, Mother, some women don't live their lives in order to please a man.''

Felicia dismissed that statement with a wave of her hand. It was an inconceivable thought, especially when she considered Brooke's career-minded focus vulgar. "Tell me about Matt Cutter. Or does he prefer to be called Matthew?''

"There's nothing to tell.'' Except that he wants to marry me. For some bizarre reason that she couldn't fathom. And she didn't plan to find out more. She certainly wasn't about to tell her mother that juicy tidbit.

In fact, maybe she'd dreamed the whole thing. Which actually seemed even more ludicrous to her. Or maybe he'd been trifling with her. A bored rich boy's game.

"He seems absolutely dreamy. Charming and deb-onaire.''

"You mean rich.'' Actually, Matt's money made her want to run the other way. Money had never made her mother content or deliriously happy. In fact, it seemed to only make her hungrier for more and set her sights on a better "catch.''

"I meant he's definitely husband material." Always mindful of calories and her waistline, Felicia delicately picked at her salad, careful not to dab too much dressing on the spinach. "He seems perfect for you."

"Why would you say that?" To Brooke, Matt was her total opposite. They were from different worlds, had different goals in life and had by some weird strike of providence been thrown together in a bizarre circumstance. It meant nothing.

Then why does your heart pound every time you think about him?

It doesn't!

But she knew it did.

Felicia set her fork on the side of the china plate and gave her daughter that direct gaze that meant *Now listen to me, young lady!* "For one thing, you could quit that job of yours."

She stared in horror at her mother. Where did she get these ideas? "Why would I want to do that? I love my job. Besides, it's not a job, it's my career. My passion. My mission."

Her mother looked as if she'd eaten something distasteful. "Passion is for candlelight and romance. Not trying to fix snotty-nosed kids' problems. I hate the fact that you have to visit those depressing places."

"Like hospitals and orphanages?"

"Precisely. They make you morose. No one wants a melancholy wife."

Brooke refrained from rolling her eyes. She wondered if Matt felt the same way about Jeffrey and the orphanage. But he hadn't appeared to look upon the small child with pity or anything else. In fact, he'd seemed perfectly at home. He'd actually asked about her patient later.

More important, would he really donate a million dollars if she agreed to marry him...or as he'd phrased it *enter into a temporary engagement?* Did money mean so little to him that he could toss it around like confetti? Or was it a way to ease his conscience for having so much when others had so little?

Not that it really mattered. She doubted she would ever see Matt Cutter again. Even if he had promised to keep in touch. What did a promise mean to him, anyway? Men like him made promises the way most people made coffee, often and without much thought. Matt's promise was probably as empty as his marriage proposal. A temporary proposal, of all things!

"Well, don't get your hopes up, Mother. I don't think I'll be seeing Mr. Cutter again." She was absolutely sure of it.

"Why on earth not? You know, Brooke, it's just as easy to fall in love with a rich man as a poor one."

"And just as easy to fall out of love, right, Mother?" Her teeth clenched in exasperation. "I don't want to fall in love at all."

"Nonsense. You don't know what you're missing." She twirled her new wedding ring around her finger. "Love is Heaven here on Earth."

"That's why you've been to divorce court so many times, right?"

"Well..." Her mother clamped her lips together.

"I'm sorry, Mother. I shouldn't have said that. But you don't seem to understand that I don't want a husband. I don't want Matt Cutter."

Liar!

* * *

"Your two-o'clock appointment has arrived, Dr. Watson," Jennifer's voice came over the intercom in her usual clipped, impersonal tone.

Brooke scanned her desk. "I don't have a file on that patient. Could you bring it in first?"

"He's new," Jennifer explained.

Releasing the tension in her neck, Brooke rotated her head to the side. She liked to be prepared for each patient. "I still need a file. What's his name?"

"Matthew Cutter."

Her heart stopped, then jolted forward like a runaway train. What was he doing here? Delivering her boots? Or was he going to propose again?

No, she'd decided she'd misunderstood him. He didn't want to marry her, temporarily or permanently, any more than she wanted him.

"He's not a patient," she said, deciding right then not to admit him to her office.

He was a nuisance.

A headache.

Definite trouble.

She pushed away from her desk and headed toward the closed door to her office that led to the reception area. She didn't know what kind of game he was playing, but she wasn't playing any longer. Before she jerked the door open, she paused to smooth the wrinkles out of her suit skirt.

God, she wished she'd taken her mother's advice and bought a new pair of shoes. Maybe with a bit more of a heel to accent her legs. And look at her hands! She could use a manicure or at least some lotion. What about her makeup? She should have at least stuck her lipstick in her purse this morning.

Are you nuts? Look at you! Primping as if you're about to meet Prince Charming!

Prince Charming, my foot. It was Matt Cutter. He was a spoiled man with obviously too much time and money on his hands.

But a good-looking man if she'd ever seen one.

What are you thinking?

Trouble was that she wasn't thinking. She was reacting, like a hormone-raging teen about to meet Ricky Martin. And she had the simple solution. She wouldn't see Matt Cutter. She'd let her secretary handle it. He could take his appointment and—

She eased open the door.

"Jennifer," she whispered, hearing the desperation in her own voice. *Self-preservation,* she corrected. "Get rid of him—"

Then her gaze met Matt's grin. Damn!

"Now, why would you want to get rid of me?" First one broad shoulder, then the other squeezed into her office. He stepped inside as if he owned the place. "After all, I did as you asked. I didn't surprise you this time. I made an appointment. And—" he checked his watch, mimicking the way she had over a week ago in the orphanage parking lot "—you owe me the next hour."

She gulped. An hour with Matt Cutter! Her heart fluttered, and she clenched her hands. She wouldn't allow him to affect her that way. Any way. "What do you want?"

He closed the door behind him and gave the bright garish decor geared more toward kids than adults a once-over. "I thought I made that clear last time. I want…need you."

Her stomach made a free-fall dive right to her

knees. She hadn't imagined his proposal. She hadn't imagined the heat, the chemistry, the attraction. Damn.

He waved his hand toward her desk. "Let me explain."

He positioned himself in front of her desk and presented his proposition as if it were a marketing deal or business acquisition. "When we first met, I remembered hearing you say your mother would love to see you married. It made me think that this could benefit you, as well."

"What are you, the fairy godmother of marriage? Marriage is not a business arrangement. It doesn't solve problems. It only complicates matters." Not that she really believed in marriage or wanted it for herself. Certainly not a marriage, even a temporary engagement to Matt Cutter.

"We won't really be getting married."

She couldn't believe she was discussing marriage, er, an engagement, logically, rationally, ridiculously with this man. Had she lost her mind, as well?

She decided to approach this as if he were a delusional patient. Not a sexy, desirable man. "Why do you want to get married, Mr. Cutter?"

"Matt. And I don't. I simply want a temporary engagement."

"Do you have a problem with marriage?"

"Not if it's the right woman. And right time. At the moment, it's undesirable. But it could make the most important woman in my life—" He got a pained expression on his handsome face. His blue eyes turned cloudy.

"Jealous?"

"Happy." His Adam's apple dipped then rose with

the strength of his resolve. The muscles along his
neck strained. "It's her last request."

Brooke felt a tightness seize her. Obviously this
meant a lot to Matt...Mr. Cutter. His raw emotion
touched her. She prided herself on being able to read
through lies and exaggerations as easily as a trans-
parent window. She knew instinctively that this was
a grave situation that mattered greatly to him.

"Who is *she?*"

"My grandmother." He averted his gaze and
seemed to straighten the wrinkles in his vulnerability.

When he looked back at her, he was the Matt Cutter the public adored—in control, decisive, invincible.
But Brooke was drawn to the tender, vulnerable side
she'd just glimpsed. She wished she'd never seen it.

"She's dying." In spite of his rock-solid, never-
give-an-inch, never-show-any-weakness manner, his
voice held a note of despair.

"Of what?"

"Everything and nothing. She's eighty-eight. She
doesn't need a specific disease. It's like she's given
up."

She nodded with understanding. "Have the doctors
given you a time frame?"

Only the strain at the corners of his mouth told her
this was a painful topic for him. "No. Could be tonight. Could be next month."

"Or next year."

"Doubtful. My grandmother is a very willful
woman. She's ready to die. And she'll get her way."

Brooke gripped the arms of her chair. His reasons
were noble, caring, sweet. But were they enough for
her to agree to his absurd proposal?

"Why me?"

"Why not you?"

"That's no answer."

He came around her desk and pulled her to her feet. Before she could protest, he wrapped his arms around her and settled her against his broad chest. A frisson of electricity ripped through her, stunned her, immobilized her. She stared up at him, unable to do the logical thing—push him away. In fact, she wanted to pull him closer. Maybe she was as crazy as he was.

"You're desirable. Sexy. Successful."

Denials lodged in her throat. She'd often heard herself described as intelligent, logical, even brilliant. She'd prided herself on those qualities. But why did she suddenly feel elated, even thrilled, by Matt's assessment?

His hand cupped her face, his fingers trailed down her throat, making her skin tingle, her toes curl inside her five-year-old sensible shoes. Why did she want to believe every word he'd said? Why did she want to seal her mouth to his? Why, oh, why, was he torturing her? A business arrangement she could handle, but his touch had turned personal, intimate, intriguing and unnerving at the same time.

Then he braced his hands on her shoulders and eased her back into her chair. Leaning over her, he aimed his steady, unaffected gaze right at her. "You're also logical, smart, kind. I thought you'd understand my predicament."

The air went out of her lungs with a whoosh. She felt light-headed, unsteady. Why did logic and intelligence suddenly sound unappealing to her?

He moved a step away from her and settled his hip on the edge of her desk. "But I also thought it would

appeal to your own needs. This kind of arrangement
might work for you, too.''

She had to admit it was tempting. For a few short
weeks her mother would be ecstatic. Then with a
swift disintegration of the engagement, Brooke could
''nurse'' her broken heart for months, maybe even
years. At least for a little while, she'd enjoy solitude,
maybe even sympathy from her mother, without her
trying to throw some guy at her every five minutes.
Ah, peace! It sounded divine.

Why didn't it seem so simple when she looked at
the situation from Matt's side? Her suspicions rose.
''How could you know it would really be beneficial
for me? You know nothing about me.''

''Not true. I know you're altruistic. You're not
money hungry.'' He grinned. ''At least not for yourself.'' He reached into his pocket for a set of keys
and tossed them onto her desk. ''The van you re-
quested.''

''A payoff?''

''Your prize instead of the roadster, remember?
Even if you would have looked great behind the
wheel. You asked for this…you got it.''

''It's that easy for you?''

''Money has its benefits.'' And drawbacks.

She fingered the keys. Why did she feel as if she'd
just sold her soul to the devil? But was he really that
awful? After all, he could have made a huge produc-
tion out of turning over this vehicle to the orphanage,
milked it for the publicity. But he hadn't.

''Thank you,'' she said. ''The kids at the orphanage will thank you, too.''

''Not needed.'' He crossed his arms over his chest.
''Look, Brooke, it's obvious that you're not interested

in my money for your own selfish gain. That's quite refreshing. Most of the women I date are out for one thing.''

''To be Mrs. Matt Cutter?''

''It is a direct path to my bank account.''

''How sad.''

''It's how the world works. But you're different. I guess I was hoping that you'd be willing to give back an engagement ring as easily as you gave away those prizes at the store.''

She smiled sheepishly. ''Now *that* I can understand.''

''Will you do it?''

She was tempted for all the right reasons...and all the wrong ones, too. ''How long would it be for?''

''Until...'' His voice dipped low, and he couldn't finish his answer. ''A month. Maybe two at the max.''

She wrestled with herself over the answer and debated whether to ask the next question. It seemed greedy. Until she thought of Jeffrey and the other kids at the orphanage. ''And were you serious about donating a million dollars to the orphanage?''

''If that's what will clench the deal between us.''

''Done, then.'' She stuck her hand out to shake on it and prayed she wasn't making a fatal error.

Matt clasped her hand and hauled her to her feet. His body collided with hers. Her mouth opened from shock. He kissed her before she could protest.

She felt his warm lips soften and meld with hers. His arms were strong, solid as they wrapped around her waist. His body felt hard. His heat melted her resistance like a lost snowflake in Texas. He stole the breath right out of her lungs, leaving her no choice but to cling to him.

Then he ended the kiss before she could fully enjoy it. Damn.

With a crooked smile that had her insides wilting beneath the wattage, he said, "Business deals end with a handshake. Engagements, even temporary ones, are sealed with a kiss."

Chapter Four

"Are you sure it's necessary for us to do this now?" Brooke asked, her mouth pinched at the corners.

"Yes," Matt answered in an equally terse tone.

He hoped she wasn't backing out on their deal. It hadn't even been twenty-four hours since they'd come to an agreement.

And what an agreement it had been. That kiss still burned in his memory and fired his blood. Why on earth had he thought he needed to kiss her?

Because…

Because they'd probably have to kiss sometime.

Because…

He'd *wanted* to kiss her.

What was wrong with that? It was natural. After all, she was a beautiful woman with eyes as deep and rich as Godiva chocolates. They melted him with each look. And what a body. She was slim and willowy with curves that begged for a man's touch and long legs that would make Cindy Crawford jealous.

But what was *his* excuse? After all, he was Matt Cutter. The tabloids liked to paint him as a playboy. Yeah, he'd dated famous models and actresses, blondes with big breasts and no brains. But he was simply a red-blooded American male. Kissing Brooke had made sense. At least in the heat of the moment. Now, still reeling from the headiness of her soft, sweet lips, it made about as much sense as leaping off the fortieth floor of his office building.

There was nothing he could do about it except try to ignore the fire she'd lit inside him and forget that she'd tasted like a mint julep. He took a surreptitious glance at her sitting next to him in his low-slung sports car. Ignoring what Brooke did to him would be more difficult than putting out a blaze with a tea-spoon of water.

He simply had to remember this was *temporary*. More so than his usual forays into the dating scene. He'd developed a strict policy of never dating a woman longer than six weeks. He'd learned the hard way that women started expecting things…like en-gagement rings, wedding bells and joint bank ac-counts.

"Damn," he said, shoving his palm against the leather-padded steering wheel. "I forgot all about an engagement ring." He never forgot details. What had Brooke done to him? Maybe it wasn't her. Maybe it was the situation with his grandmother's health.

"Don't worry about it. I don't wear jewelry." Brooke smoothed a lock of brown hair behind her dainty ear and touched a tiny diamond stud. It was a simple, tasteful earring rather than an extravagant and garish piece of jewelry. "Well, except for these. But they're special."

"How so?"

She gazed out the side window. "They were a gift."

From whom? An old boyfriend? Lover? Ex-husband? His abdomen tightened with irritation. What did it matter? He wasn't interested in Brooke for anything other than this simple mission that would make his grandmother happy. So he refused to ask the obvious question that burned in his gut.

Instead, he asked, "You wouldn't even wear an engagement ring if you were really getting married?"

She shrugged. "I don't see the point."

He shouldn't have been surprised by her disinterest in jewelry. After all, she gave away cars and money the way most of the women he knew gave away an out-of-season wardrobe. A closer look at the woman sitting next to him made him realize she didn't need jewelry or a lot of makeup. She looked stunning without all the ornamentation that so many women relied on.

"What about a wedding ring? Wouldn't you want something flashy to show off to your girlfriends? Or to ward off unwanted advances from men?"

She looked at him as if he'd suddenly spoken in a foreign language. "If I were to ever say those solemn vows to anyone, I wouldn't need a ring to make them any more real or precious."

Her answer dumbfounded him. All the women he'd ever known delighted in one-upping their friends with iceberg-size diamonds, luxurious furs and grandiose mansions. All provided by their rich husbands. Except for his grandmother. Could Brooke fall into that very rare and very special category?

"Why couldn't we wait a week or so to make the announcement?" Brooke asked, jarring him out of his uncomfortable thoughts. Her right hand gripped the door as though she might make a break for it at the next stoplight.

"We might not have a week." Fear clamped around his heart. "My grandmother is gravely ill. I'm doing this for her, remember? For her last wish."

She nodded, her features looking taut. Straightening a wrinkle out of her no-nonsense skirt, she skimmed her hand down her thigh, which put a crease in his plan to forget the way her body had felt against his. He shifted gears, trying to keep his mind on driving and on his reasons for being temporarily engaged, and *off* Brook.

"What's wrong?" he asked, noticing her fidgeting.

"We're not prepared. We don't have our stories straight. So to speak."

"What's there to know? It's not like we're trying to cover up a crime. We're engaged. What's there to know?"

"Like where we met. How we fell in love? When—"

"We met at the store when you became our millionth customer. I told my grandmother then that you were…" *Don't go there.*

"What?"

"Never mind." He grinned, remembering how she'd shattered his preconceived notions of a woman out shopping. "I told her how you gave away all my prizes."

"Not all," she said, humor making her brown eyes glow mischievously. "When do I get my boots?"

"Relax, Cinderella, you'll get them."

The smooth skin between her brows pinched in a frown. "Back to our story."

He nodded tersely and gripped the steering wheel sternly. "We met again when I delivered the van to the orphanage. And we fell in love."

"That fast?"

"Simple as that. Don't make it more complicated than it has to be."

She blew out a puff of air. "Everything about this is complicated. You must not know much about love, because it's the most complicated emotion."

"Not when it's right." Or so he'd heard his whole life from his grandmother. But love and marriage had always seemed way too confusing for him. So he'd managed to steer clear. His gaze locked with hers for a sizzling second that rattled his nerves. He cleared his throat and stared straight ahead at the road. Not at Brooke. Not at her long, sexy legs or her perceptive eyes. Not at her wide, sensuous mouth.

"Don't overanalyze it," he said, his voice steady and calm, even though he felt he was slowly spinning out of control. And he didn't like it. "No one else will. Everyone will assume it was just a matter of time before some woman caught me."

"Caught you?" Her voice lifted. "You mean people will think I trapped you?"

The panic-stricken look on her face made him scramble for a better answer. "I didn't mean it that way."

"I did not chase you. Nor did I set out to trap you, if that's what you think."

"Whoa, darlin', this isn't real. We're *not* engaged. If it'll make you feel better I'll say you gave me a run for my money."

"What's that supposed to mean? That I was after your fortune?"

"No." He shoved his fingers through his hair. She was exasperating. "I'll say you weren't interested in dating me, but I managed to change your mind. You just couldn't resist my charm." He gave her his best smile and hoped it had the magic that all the magazines touted.

She slanted her gaze toward him and after a long pause, said, "Okay. I guess that'll be okay."

But he wasn't sure anymore. He tried to sort through his thoughts but realized Brooke made him feel off balance. He shrugged off the unusual sensation and concentrated on his driving. He had to remember this was business. There wasn't any reason for them to get emotionally involved. But already he felt confused and ready to run.

"Wait a minute," she said, her fingers flexing as if she was putting on the brakes. "'No one.' 'Everyone.' Who are these people that are going to know about the engagement? Just your grandmother…your family, right?"

He shrugged. "Maybe."

She turned a doubtful gaze on him. "Who else?"

"I am a national celebrity. The press is—"

"The press?" she shrieked.

"They're naturally curious. They say I sell papers and magazines."

"Oh, God," she moaned, and put her head in her hands. "Maybe we should rethink this."

"Too late," he said, "we're here." He zipped into

a parking space, killed the motor and shifted in his seat.

He realized his sporty Mercedes was way too snug. He was far too close to Brooke. He could smell her light, airy fragrance that reminded him of a cool, refreshing ocean breeze with the sun glittering off dazzling, white sandy beaches. Damn. He should have chosen a luxury model car instead of this two-seater.

"Look," he said, pretending this was a business acquisition instead of an engagement. A fake engagement. "It'll all work out. Remember, it's only temporary. I'll do all I can—"

"You've done enough." Her gaze met his, and her chin lifted. "I've been thinking about that kiss."

"Yeah?" He gave his voice a suggestive lilt. His gut tightened with heightened awareness. "And what have you been thinking? That you'd like to give it another try?"

"No. N-no." Her eyes widened with dismay, and she leaned back against the car door. "That's not what I meant at all."

Crossing his arms over his chest, he felt disappointment race through his veins. "What did you mean?"

"Nothing."

"So, what about the kiss is bothering you?" Because everything was bothering him—from his blatant reaction to the reason why he'd kissed her in the first place.

"I guess," she said, her gaze slipping away from him to stare at the hood of his car, "we'll be expected—as an engaged couple, of course, even though it's all pretend—to kiss. Once in a while."

"Seems the logical thing to do." Yet at the same time irrational. At least for his libido. But he couldn't help anticipating the next kiss with Brooke. "Do you have a problem with kissing me? Was it that distasteful?" The idea seemed ludicrous. He'd never had any complaints before. What was it with this woman?

"No, I mean, yes…that is…"

He noted a heated stain darken her cheeks. Her flustered state calmed his concern and amused him. So maybe that kiss had surprised and aroused her, too. Interesting. Definitely interesting.

It's neither, Cutter, it's just plain stupid. Remember, this is only temporary. "Three," she said, jerking him out of his internal argument.

"Excuse me?"

"I think we should limit the kisses to three."

"Three kisses?"

"Yes." Her features seemed to relax. "And only when it's necessary. Only when others are present. Only when—"

"I don't know if all these rules are necessary or even possible."

"They are." Her chin squared with determination.

"What are we going to say when someone says, 'Aren't you going to kiss your bride-to-be?' 'No, sorry, we've already had our allotted three for the day.'"

She rolled her lips inward and contemplated his question. "Of course not. But the rule of three is for us to…"

"Control ourselves?" He grinned.

"Yes."

"Fine." He drew his finger down her cheek. They'd kiss again. And he'd make damn sure it knocked her socks off. "Just remember rules were made to be broken."

* * *

Feeling less in control of this crazy situation and her own reactions to Matt, Brooke walked alongside him as they entered the hospital, making sure their hands didn't brush or their shoulders touch. Her nerves felt frayed, her skin electrified. What was she going to do about him? Better yet, how was she going to get her responses to his touch...his kiss...under control?

She was curiously and irritatingly aware of others watching them. More specifically—him. Every pair of female eyes seemed to trail after Matt as if he was a Greek god. But he wasn't. He was flesh and blood. A man. That's all.

But what a man! Who sure could kiss!

Stop it, Brooke. Don't get all gaga over him. It was just a kiss. Forget it.

But she didn't think she could. Especially if they had to kiss again. Which seemed inevitable. Her knees trembled in anticipation.

Get a grip, Brooke! And forget him.

After this charade was over, they would go their separate ways all right. He'd head back to his jet-setting life, flitting from woman to woman, while she would happily settle back into her shell and continue with her work. But she would never forget Matt.

He wasn't like any other man she'd ever met. Why that bothered her, she wasn't sure. But she would prefer it if she could categorize him. Then she would understand him. But damn if he fit any of her pre-conceived notions.

"Here we go," he said, grasping her hand. His touch was warm and had a steadying effect on the questions zinging around her mind. At the same time he made her dizzy; her pulse accelerated and her skin grew taut.

Oh, heavens! What had she agreed to? As they entered the hospital room, she had the strangest sense that Matt wasn't holding her hand to enhance their engagement story. It seemed more personal. As though he somehow needed her support.

She gave his hand a tiny squeeze of encouragement. "For better or worse."

His tense features relaxed into one of his curl-your-toes smiles. Shocked by the intensity, Brooke jerked her gaze away from him.

She focused on the frail woman lying in the hospital bed. She had a cloud of white curls about her face. Her skin looked as thin as parchment. But her deep-blue eyes reminded her of Matt. Yet they lacked the power and passion his created.

"Hello, darlin'," he said, walking straight for the patient.

Brooke felt like dragging her feet. How could she lie to this fragile woman? She looked like a part of her had already died and only the shell remained.

"Who's this?" his grandmother cut to the chase. Her voice held more strength and determination than Brooke believed her feeble body could possess.

"Brooke Watson." She held out her hand. "It's a pleasure to meet you."

"Then I guess you know I'm Eliza Cutter," she said, touching her hand to Brooke's. "I'm sure you've heard all about me." Her skin felt cool to the touch, but the deep chill came from her piercing gaze that she turned on her grandson. "Matt, I'm ashamed of you."

"Why's that?" He sat on the bed as if he weren't concerned in the least about her admonishment.

"I told you not to get me a shrink. This is not in my head. It's in my bones. In my weak blood. It's just time for me to go. Now it's time for you to face facts."

Matt tipped his head back and laughed. "How'd you know Brooke was a psychologist?"

"I'm eighty-eight years old," she said as if that explained everything.

Brooke glanced from grandmother to grandson. "I didn't come here on official business, Mrs. Cutter."

"Oh?" Suspicious, Eliza slanted a questioning gaze at Matt.

"She's right. I didn't bring her to talk you into living one day longer than you want. I learned a long time ago that once your mind is made up, that's it. So I'm not going to even try."

"Good." Eliza crossed her arms over her chest. "Then why's a psychologist here if not to analyze my mental state?"

"Actually, she's a child psychologist." He slipped his arm around Brooke's waist.

His fingers, firm and arousing, pressed into her flesh. She felt her stomach dip low, and a heady rush of blood surged through her. His gaze locked with hers, and she knew what was coming. He was going to kiss her. No doubt about it.

She should dread it. She should put a hand against his chest and keep her distance. But she couldn't move. She could only watch him tilt his face and then feel his warm lips capture hers briefly.

"One," he whispered against her mouth before pulling back. Then, shifting his focus back to his grandmother, he dismissed Brooke as if he were simply toying with her, as if the kiss hadn't affected him in any way.

She clenched her hands to try to control the titillating vibrations coursing through her body. Her senses felt overwhelmed, as if they'd been shocked by an electrical current. She would have pulled away from him, but his arm around her waist became a resistant band that kept her firmly against his side.

"Grandmother," Matt explained, "Brooke is the woman who was our millionth customer."

"Oh-h-h?" The older woman blinked, and suddenly a spark entered her eyes. She sharpened her gaze on Brooke. "Really?"

"I'm the one," Brooke said, offering a smile.

Suddenly Eliza beamed. Her cheeks brightened, and her terse lips spread into a wide smile. "Well, well, well." She tilted her head to the side and studied Brooke. "The exasperating one. Matt, you said you couldn't remember what she looked like. If that's true then you're closer to death than I am."

Matt gave Brooke a wink that tied her insides into knots. "I was in denial then."

"And you think she's beautiful now?"

"Absolutely," he answered. This time he dipped his head and kissed her neck, making her skin flutter. "Two," he whispered for only her to hear.

Heat rippled through her abdomen. He was going to push her to the edge, just as he was going to push the rules she'd established.

She elbowed him to give herself some breathing room. "You said I was exasperating?"

"Among other things."

"How about if I give you an assessment?"

He grinned. "Anytime, Doc. Anytime."

Eliza leaned back against her fluffed pillows and closed her eyes with a sigh.

"What's the matter, Grandmother?" Matt asked, alarm sharpening his features. His body tensed.

"Not a thing," Eliza breathed.

"Are you tired?" he asked.

"Maybe we should go," Brooke suggested.

Eliza shook her head. "I was simply saying a prayer of thanksgiving."

"For what?" Matt asked, confusion crinkling his forehead.

"Well, I won't steal your thunder." She opened her eyes and studied them. Then, with a wave of her hand, she said, "Go ahead. Spill the beans."

"About what?" Matt asked.

"You said you brought this young woman here for another reason besides trying to outsmart me or have me committed." Eliza looked as if the news could either devastate her or buoy her up. "So is it you, Matt, who's about to finally commit?"

"I never could keep a secret from you, could I?" He cleared his throat as if preparing for a grand speech. "Grandmother, we're going to be married."

"I knew it!" Eliza clapped her hands. "Hallelujah!"

Matt pulled Brooke closer, and his mouth hovered over hers. "Three," he said before he kissed her soundly, his mouth covering hers, his warmth overpowering her.

Her ears rang from the sudden rush of blood pumping through her veins. She should be angry, irritated at him. But she wasn't. She should want to push him away. But she didn't. She wanted to pull him closer, kiss him more fully. His kisses weren't annoying her; they were frustrating her. Because she wanted more!

Oh, heavens! How many more kisses would she have to endure? How many more would she have to try to forget?

Chapter Five

"Come here, dear," Eliza beckoned to her, her voice sincere with a mild Texas accent.

It gave Brooke a much-needed excuse to step away from Matt, his dizzying effect on her and her confusing feelings. She hoped she didn't stumble, because Matt's touch had made her knees weak and her nerves jittery.

Barely able to think clearly after his three kisses, Brooke wondered why his grandmother had so easily accepted his announcement. She hadn't even questioned the suddenness of their engagement or probed further into Brooke's character. Feeling awkward and wary, she moved toward the older woman's hospital bed.

Eliza Cutter was too sharp to believe such nonsense as this fairy-tale engagement. Or was she? Maybe she so wanted her grandson married that all her sound reasoning was dwarfed by her imminent joy. Guilt made Brooke's skin burn with regret for the lies they were telling, and she couldn't meet the older woman's gaze.

"Welcome to the family, my dear." Eliza clasped Brooke's hands and pulled her forward, pressing her cheek against Brooke's. "Congratulations." Her hands were still cold, but there was a warmth to her touch and vibrancy to her voice now. "I hope you know you're getting a wonderful man."

She was not getting Matt. Wonderful or not.

"I hope you two will be as happy as Linc and I were. We had over fifty wonderful years together. I'm so delighted for you both." Eliza's sharp gaze focused on Brooke. "I can see that my grandson adores you. The way he looks at you and kisses you every chance he can. Well, it makes my heart flutter when I remember the way Linc used to grab me and kiss me. We never could get enough of each other."

Brooke's throat clogged with a myriad of emotions she hadn't expected and couldn't deny. Her mother certainly had never spoken of one of her many husbands that way. But her father had once only had eyes for Felicia. It widened the crack in her own heart that her father's love for her mother had withered and died. Their love had not been a mutual till-death-do-we-part kind, only a passing fancy for Felicia...until the next, better man came along.

But Eliza Cutter's obvious love for her deceased husband gave Brooke a spark of hope. Maybe love could endure. Maybe, just maybe...

She cut her thoughts short. It was the love Eliza still felt for her husband that brought hope to Brooke's heart. Not Matt. Not his kisses. Not the way he looked at her.

From the corner of her eye she was too aware of

Matt watching her, studying her. His gaze was intense and determined. Before he could move to kiss her again, she stepped away. Her nerves already felt tattered.

"Matt," she said, "give your grandmother a kiss."

"Come here, you big lug." Eliza clasped Matt to her, clapping him on the back. "You've made an old woman very happy. I'm thrilled for you. Just thrilled."

Matt cradled his grandmother tenderly against his chest, making Brooke's heart contract. Over the older woman's shoulder, he mouthed to Brooke, "Thank you."

Her heart pounded out its doubts. Had they done the right thing? She'd never encouraged a patient to lie. But maybe this little white one would prove to be helpful instead of hurtful.

His grandmother certainly looked happy. Their announcement had taken years off her face and somehow eased the pain and infirmity that had ravaged her body.

But could Brooke live with the deception? And could she walk away from Matt without a backward glance or wishful hope? For an odd moment she wished it wasn't a lie at all. Which startled her.

Eliza sniffed away her joyful tears. "There's not much time now. We've got to get busy planning."

"Oh, Grandmother. Let's not worry about that yet. Let's just enjoy the moment. We're not in any hurry."

"Not in a hurry!" Eliza tsked. "I remember how impatient young love is. Why, your grandfather and I couldn't wait to be married. But then that was in the olden days when you didn't sleep together before marriage."

"Grandmother!"

Brooke's cheeks burned, and she refused to look at Matt. She didn't want to think about making love to him. It was enough that she couldn't forget his kisses. If they ever did make love, she knew she'd be a goner.

"Oh, don't 'grandmother' me." Eliza pursed her lips.

Unable to resist the magnetic pull of Matt's gaze, Brooke felt a spark simmer between them. It made her tense and restless with a raw need she'd rarely, if ever, felt. Actually, she couldn't remember a boyfriend ever making her feel giddy and at the same filled with longing. It shattered her composure.

Even though they hadn't made love, Brooke felt oddly joined with Matt. Maybe it was the sympathy she felt for him and his grandmother in this difficult situation. Or maybe it was those darn kisses. Heat suffused her skin, making her tingle from head to toe.

"But there's nothing like marital bliss," Eliza said. "And what I wouldn't do to see you two married…before my time is up." She straightened the sheet atop her lap. "So, let's get started. When's the date?"

"The date?" Matt asked.

"For the wedding."

He met Brooke's panicked gaze. "Uh…darlin'…" He reached for her hand. "We haven't chosen a date yet, have we?"

"No." Brooke's throat felt tight.

"Well, if there's no special date in mind, nothing that you're attached to, then let's set one right now." Eliza clasped her gnarled hands in her lap. "How about one month from this Saturday?"

"Uh…uh," Matt stammered.

"One month?" Brooke repeated, a numbness rushing over her. She looked to Matt for help, but obviously he didn't know how to say no to his grandmother. Which was how they'd ended up in this predicament in the first place. "That's really not enough time to get everything planned."

"Sure it is."

"But there's so much to do. What if…" Her brain faltered, trying to come up with reasons. What went into planning a wedding, anyway? She should have taken notes during all of her mother's.

"It takes time to reserve a place for the wedding. Doesn't it?" She looked toward Matt.

"Sure. We need a reception site, too," Matt added, coming to her defense.

Together they nodded. Brooke felt a sense of pleasure at how well they worked together.

"Nonsense." Eliza deflated their excuse with her response. "The location doesn't matter. You could get married in a barn. When your grandfather and I married, all we could see was each other. The place didn't matter at all."

How could they argue with that? If they did, then Eliza might suspect they weren't truly in love.

"There's a sweet little spot that you might consider. But if it's not available, you could always get married at the estate. There's plenty of room and lots of help." Eliza clasped her hands. "So that's settled."

"B-but…" Matt protested.

"What about the cake?" Brooke asked, excuses piling up in her mind. "And food for the reception?

I'm sure all the best caterers are booked solid for months and months.''

"We can always work something out with our personal chef. I'm sure André will take care of it.''

Damn. Brooke gritted her teeth. She suspected Eliza Cutter had been secretly planning Matt's wedding for years.

"I'm sure Brooke has something special in mind for her dress,'' Matt pointed out.

"Yes,'' Brooke said lamely, feeling suddenly depleted of all energy. But what? She scrambled to imagine herself in a wedding dress. What type would she want, anyway? Something simple. Something elegant. Something traditional, like the vows.

No, no, no! She wasn't supposed to imagine herself as a bride. Even temporarily. She'd spent her whole life avoiding something like this…someone like Matt. But it was less than a week since she'd met him, and he had her engaged and planning a wedding. What had he done to her?

"You could always borrow someone's dress,'' Eliza suggested. "Doesn't your mother still have her wedding dress?''

"About a dozen, actually,'' Brooke answered, her thoughts still mulling over the incredulity that she could envision herself in a champagne-colored wedding dress walking down the aisle. Toward Matt. What was wrong with her?

Matt stared at her. And Brooke knew she'd made a fatal error.

"See!'' Eliza beamed. "No problem then with a dress. It's agreed.'' She held out her hands to each of them. Slowly they formed a united, if not reluctant, circle. "Don't worry about a thing, Brooke. I'll help you with all the tiny details."

"But—"

"Grandmother—"

"Oh, don't worry. I won't step on the bride's toes. Every decision will be hers. I'll simply be the facilitator."

"Coordinator," Matt supplied.

Dumbfounded, Brooke stared at him.

"Good, then it's decided." Eliza's eyes filled with tears. "I've got to call my doctor and get out of this hospital. We've got work to do! My dear grandson is going to be married."

"Why didn't you do something?" Brooke demanded the second they reached the hospital lobby and the shock had faded into confusion.

Her tone and demeanor irked him. What was he supposed to do? Give his grandmother a joyous thrill one minute, then break her heart the next? "Why didn't you?"

"What was I supposed to do?" she challenged.

"I don't know. Say you weren't ready. Say you had a designer in mind for the dress and it would take years to find all the beads or grow the worms for the perfect silk. Anything but that you had access to a dozen of your mother's wedding dresses."

She scowled at him.

He wondered then about a woman who had that many wedding dresses. "Your mother's been married a dozen times?"

"Seems like that. But I lose count." She gave a slight shake of her head. "That's not the point. Why didn't you say the carpets at the estate would have to be cleaned? Or that there was a fire yesterday and the whole place burned to the ground? You didn't help, either.''

''I couldn't disappoint her.'' Strange emotions that he didn't recognize clamped around his heart. ''She looked so happy.''

Brooke's mouth thinned. ''You have to tell her.''

''How would you suggest I break her heart?'' Matt countered.

That silenced her. Long enough for him to try to think of a way out of this predicament. Why hadn't he anticipated this? Why hadn't he foreseen that his grandmother would naturally want to see the wedding take place?

Had Brooke clouded his better judgment? Absolutely not. No woman had ever done such an absurd thing. And no woman ever would.

The answer was simple. He'd been too distraught about his grandmother's health to think clearly. He hadn't believed she was strong enough to even suggest helping with the wedding, much less attending it. He'd been focused on making her happy. That was all.

But now it wasn't enough. Now he had to produce a wedding. Now he had to marry Brooke!

A cold sweat broke out on his brow. Nothing ever made him lose his cool, not spending millions on a risky business deal, not facing a roomful of overeager reporters or even a boardroom of uptight and over-educated lawyers. What was wrong with him?

''We'll just have to go through with it,'' he stated simply, firmly, decisively, even though his nerves shivered at the prospect.

''What?'' she shrieked, gaining the attention of

several hospital personnel walking past them toward the bank of elevators.

"We're being watched," he warned.

"I don't care if we're being filmed. We are not getting married."

"But—"

She didn't stick around to listen to his excuses. She walked right out the revolving door. But he wasn't about to let her get away. Not yet, anyway.

"It's our only option," he said, catching up to her.

The sharp rays of the sun made him squint. The heat made his shirt stick to his back. Or was it the possibility of getting married…marrying Brooke… that had him sweating? Or worse, the chance that Brooke would refuse and walk out of his life as easily as she'd walked into it?

"That's too bad because we're not…. I'm not accepting it."

He had to change her mind. For his grandmother's sake, of course. "What's wrong? You think you'd be stuck with me forever?"

"Forever doesn't scare me. Temporary does."

He frowned. "Because of your mother and all her marriages?"

"I am not the topic under discussion," she said, carefully untangling herself from a more intimate discussion. "Our marriage…or nonwedding is the problem." She crossed her arms over her chest. "Now what are we going to do?"

"Get married," he said, knowing that was the only answer. "Temporarily. We'll have it annulled later. After—"

"No way. I'm not going to become my mother."

The determination in her voice filled him with admiration and anger.

At least she didn't take marriage lightly. She was different from most of the women he knew, who would marry for money and hope for love later. But damn she was exasperating!

Suddenly his clothes felt constricting. Brooke's principles were too appealing. Too dangerous. If she'd been like any other woman, he could easily dismiss her, forget about her. But he couldn't. And he knew then it was more than her soft kisses that had him tied into knots.

"We can't make it a permanent arrangement," he said, determined not to get carried away with this farce.

"Of course not," she agreed.

Her statement felt like a rejection, disgruntling him. But he didn't stop to analyze why. It didn't matter. He should be relieved that she didn't want to really marry him. He liked being single. He wasn't ready for marriage.

Then why did he suddenly feel all alone in the world?

"So what do you suggest?" he asked, unable to think clearly.

"We'll have to break up."

He frowned. He didn't like the sound of that. But he knew it was the only answer. "How will that help my grandmother?"

"It won't. But she'll believe you're interested in finding love and capable of committing. Maybe that will give her solace. Mostly, though, it will keep us from confessing it was all an elaborate, if not very well thought out, plan to deceive her."

It made sense. Or did it? Doubts and concerns surfaced. "What if she starts talking about dying again?"

"Then maybe she needs psychiatric help. You saw the change in her after you announced our engagement. If she was truly ill our news wouldn't have had that profound an effect on her condition."

"How can I be sure?" He jammed his hands into his pants pockets. He wouldn't jeopardize his grandmother's health. But he also wasn't comfortable with the fact that he would have to let Brooke go sooner or later. It made no sense. "I can't assume she'll be okay. She could suffer a real relapse."

"Maybe you should talk to her doctor."

"I will." Another idea took root. "In the meantime, we need to continue our charade."

"Why?"

"Just to be sure she's on the road to recovery." Yes, that was the reason. It had nothing to do with him or Brooke or the way she made him feel. "Then when my grandmother seems healthier and stronger, we'll break up and go our separate ways." Later. Much later.

"I don't know," she said, hedging. "This has to end sometime."

But did it? It was an irrational thought, same as wanting to kiss Brooke, and he shoved both ideas aside. He decided at that moment he would avoid kissing her from now on. Obviously her kisses had some weird side effect on him, like a bad reaction to a flu shot.

"Of course," he agreed. "It will end. But at a more appropriate time." He just didn't want to think about when. "We'll begin planning the wedding."

"I don't know," she said, her eyes narrowing.

Feeling more was on the line than his grandmother's health, he pressed further. "Our different tastes and preferences will show everyone that we're not suited for each other."

"Possibly." Then her eyes brightened. "That might work."

"Sure it will." He grinned, relieved they'd come to an understanding. At least she hadn't run out on him. Not yet, anyway.

She stepped back suddenly. "Don't even think about it."

Confused, he asked, "What?"

"Sealing the deal with a kiss."

"Wouldn't dream of it." But he would. He had. But it was better if they didn't kiss anymore. "I've already had my allotted three for the day."

"I can't believe we're doing this," Brooke whispered aloud, staring out the side window of the Cutters' chauffeur-driven Bentley.

"Neither can I." Matt gave her shoulder a warning squeeze. "Exciting, isn't it?" he tried to cover her gaffe.

Unnerving actually. "Uh, yeah."

Happy to be out of the hospital, Eliza nodded. Her eyes glittered with anticipation, her fingers drummed with nervous energy against her purse lying across her lap. "Indeed. There's nothing like planning a wedding. I remember as if it were yesterday when Linc and I started planning ours. What a joyous time in our lives. And it will be for you, too."

Brooke doubted that. After all, this planning phase, according to the new plan, was supposed to accentuate their differences. And she and Matt were different.

He was hard where she was soft. She gave herself a mental shake. She meant, he was hardheaded. And she'd gone soft in the head to agree to this.

There were more incompatibilities. She followed the rules, whereas he enjoyed bending them. Like the limit on kisses. She'd learned the hard way not to impose something like that on Matt again.

And he didn't take marriage seriously. After all, he was willing to marry her to make his grandmother happy. What kind of commitment was that? Not the kind she was interested in.

"How are you feeling today, Eliza?" Brooke asked, trying to fill the silence in the overpriced, overindulgent car that would have had her mother salivating.

"Chipper now that I'm out of the hospital." Eliza had done exactly as she'd stated. She'd called her doctor and insisted that he release her. She'd been home that afternoon. The next morning, she'd called her grandson and insisted they start searching for a suitable place for the wedding ceremony.

"You let us know if you get too tired," he stated as if he wore a white medical coat.

"Don't you worry about me." She patted her grandson's thigh. "You just look after your fiancée's needs."

Matt sat between the two women. He wore a crisp white button-down and khaki pants. He didn't have to wear a tuxedo to attract attention. He commanded it no matter what he wore. He didn't even have to kiss Brooke to grab her attention.

He leaned toward her, his breath warm against her

neck, as he whispered, "My pleasure. Or should I say, what's yours?"

A kiss, she thought. Brooke swallowed hard. What was the matter with her? She didn't want to kiss him.

Actually she realized then that she didn't want the charade to end. She didn't like pretending. She hated lying. But she wanted to go right on kissing Matt. Which was a perplexing and startling realization.

Of course, it was understandable from the physiological aspect. He was handsome, sexy and the best kisser. She would admit only to herself that her experience was limited to a handful of men, but if there were a contest, Matt would win.

Despite the physiological needs coursing through her system, she reminded herself that she didn't have room in her life for a man. Especially one like Matt. He would naturally fit all her mother's criteria for the perfect prospective husband. But he didn't match Brooke's.

If she ever contemplated marriage, or even a relationship with a man, it would have to be with someone who could commit. And Matt Cutter wasn't the type. Why, every other week, there was a picture of him in a tabloid or on the society pages of the *San Antonio Gazette* escorting a gorgeous blonde, brunette or redhead to some extravaganza. She would not be another notch on his cummerbund.

Needing to get her mind off these ridiculous thoughts, she leaned forward and looked toward Eliza. Just the break in contact from Matt's hand to her shoulder helped placate her jumbled nerves. "Where are you taking us?"

"I thought we'd take a look at a quaint chapel on the outskirts of San Antonio, since you both agreed

you wanted a small wedding.'' Eliza gave them both
a smile as if approving their decision.

Matt and Brooke had agreed beforehand to disagree. But that's not how it had worked out. Brooke
had said she wanted a small, intimate ceremony with
only family and their closest friends. With a secretive
smile, Eliza had said, ''Isn't that what you've always
said you wanted, too, Matt?'' He'd had to admit it
was the truth. So much for their plan.

Now they'd have to disagree about this chapel.

Eliza strained her neck to peer out the side window
at the passing vehicles and desert landscape. ''It
won't be long now.''

Brooke's gaze followed the older woman's. Trees
were scarce in this part of the country, as were bushes
and wildflowers. But there was plenty of brush, making the terrain look harsh and uncivilized. She liked
this part of Texas, enjoyed the heat, and the rich heritage and glorious history appealed to her senses and
down-to-earth nature.

Thirty minutes later the Bentley, looking out of
place among the cacti and sage, turned down a narrow
dirt road. After weaving its way into a cavern, it finally came to a stop near an adobe mission. The
chauffeur opened the door and helped first Eliza and
then Brooke out of the car.

The afternoon sun felt hot and unrelenting as its
rays reflected off the sandy patches. What grass had
once grown here had turned brown and brittle. But
there was a beauty in the harshness, a promise in the
sunlight and azure sky, that gave Brooke's senses a
jolt. Beside the arched doorway leading inside the
mission, bougainvillea bloomed bright and colorful in
a dazzling array of yellows and pinks. It gave the

chapel a magical quality, as if anything touching this place would be transformed.

"It dates back to the eighteenth century," Eliza stated as she picked her way across the pebbles and rocks.

Matt took her arm, helping her and making sure she didn't stumble or fall. His attentiveness to his grandmother touched Brooke, made her even more aware that this was a special, caring man.

"The Indians said it was a mystical place. I think it's magical." Eliza sounded breathless, but Brooke realized it wasn't from exertion so much as from excitement. "The Spaniards had to abandon it not long after it was built. But it survived Santa Anna's armies, droughts and Indian raids. The Historical Society owns it now and keeps it restored."

With Matt at her side, Eliza stepped inside, the darkness swallowing them. Brooke followed into the surprising coolness, and her breath snagged in her throat.

"It's amazing," she said, her voice echoing in the stillness.

"Isn't it?" Eliza nodded. "What do you think, Matt?"

His silence drew Brooke's gaze. This was a golden opportunity for them to disagree. For their differences to appear. For them to even argue. Now that she'd made her preference known, she expected him to object. But he didn't. He remained silent, his brow furrowed.

"What's wrong?" she asked. Hoping to prod him, she added, "You don't like it, do you?"

"I didn't say that."

His answer sent a suspicious chill down her spine.

While Eliza's back was turned, Brooke poked him in the side. She tilted her head, trying to silently remind him of their plan. That he was supposed to argue, to dissent, to do something to get them out of this wedding.

"I can't imagine we'd be able to book this chapel," he finally said. "The waiting list must be long."

"I already checked," Eliza said, her eyes glimmering with unshed tears. "It's available if you want it."

Matt glanced at Brooke. "What do you think, darlin'?"

What could she say now? No? She'd already committed. Or she should be committed for agreeing to this charade. "Well...I, um..."

"It makes you speechless, doesn't it?" Eliza said, her voice warbling. "That's exactly how Linc and I felt when we discovered it."

The realization hit Brooke like a two-by-four. "You were married here, weren't you?"

Eliza sniffed into her linen handkerchief. "Fifty-eight years ago." She stepped back and pushed Brooke and Matt together.

His arm automatically came around her. A warmth zapped the strength from her legs.

"I hope it will bring you a long, happy life together," Eliza whispered as if in prayer.

Brooke's gaze reluctantly met Matt's. A tremor rippled through her abdomen, and her skin prickled with awareness. "We're one step closer to our wedding."

Instead of taking her statement as a dire warning, he bent his head toward hers. "We are, aren't we?"

"Well..." Eliza said impatiently.

"What?" Matt asked, pausing before he kissed her again.

Her heart pounded against her rib cage. She should push him away. But she couldn't find the strength to resist him. Dammit, she wanted him to kiss her.

"Aren't you going to kiss your future bride?" Eliza asked impatiently.

Giving Brooke a look that said he had no choice, he leaned forward, his breath bathing her mouth, making her eager for his kiss, long for it. What was wrong with her? Why couldn't she stop her pulse from galloping with need?

She decided not to fight him this time, not to fight the desire. Instead, she closed her eyes, lifted her chin to fully accommodate him and parted her lips with anticipation.

"No," he said, his voice raw as if he were making a painful decision. His simple statement slammed her heart closed.

She popped her eyes open and met his heated gaze. Confusion jumbled her thoughts, not to mention the heat spiraling through her, grazing her cheeks, making her want to crawl under the nearest pew.

No? No! What did he mean?

"No," he repeated, "I won't kiss you. Not this time."

Chapter Six

"No?" his grandmother repeated, giving a disapproving snort.

Brooke's brow furrowed. She actually looked disappointed, making Matt regret his sudden, irrational decision not to kiss her.

She took a step backward out of his embrace. "No?"

Her incredulous tone made him curse himself. She sounded as though she'd *wanted* to kiss him. Her lips had parted and her eyes had closed as if she'd *craved* it as much as he had.

That's why he'd refused.

"No," he said, reaffirming his decision.

He had to stop wanting her. It was not healthy. It would not put the much-needed distance between them. And he desperately needed some distance to get his libido and his emotions under control.

Obviously she'd been as affected by the chapel as he had been. He'd sensed it. Neither had been able to deny their reactions or argue the way they'd planned. Especially after they both realized it was the place his grandparents had been married. He refused to admit they had similar tastes.

The weight of Brooke's glare and his grandmother's confused stare chafed against him. Brooke crossed her arms beneath her breasts, making the soft material stretch over them and remind him of what he'd missed by not kissing her. Was she miffed that he'd refused to kiss her? His grandmother shook her head as if confounded by young people these days. He had to explain his reason for not kissing his bride.

But he couldn't say he *wanted* her. He couldn't say a part of him had needed that kiss, needed Brooke. No, he needed an excuse and he needed it quick.

"I, um, I don't think we should kiss."

"Ever?" his grandmother asked.

Brooke arched one eyebrow at him. Okay, she'd limited him once to three kisses. Now she welcomed his kiss? Demanded it? What was she doing to him? Tying him in knots, that's what.

Get a grip, Cutter. She's simply trying to stay in character—that of a bride-to-be.

"I mean, here," he said, grabbing the first rational thought that flicked through his brain. "I don't think we should kiss…here…in this mission."

Suddenly Brooke's lip curled with amusement. She was enjoying his predicament, wasn't she? "I don't think God has anything against kissing."

"Of course not," Eliza said. "After all, He invented it."

Matt felt each second click off impatiently as they waited for him to explain further. "I mean…in this special place. We should only kiss here…"

His gaze shifted from the altar at the front to collide with Brooke's. Man, oh, man, he wanted to kiss her right now. A deep, wet kiss that would go on and on and on. Uninterrupted. Without an audience. Just Brooke and him. Alone. Together.

"Once," he said, needing air. "On our wedding day."

Brooke's lips tightened as if weighing his answer.

"How sweet," Eliza answered, erasing her disapproval with a smile. "It will create a truly magical moment. You've got yourself a romantic husband, Brooke."

"Uh-huh," she mumbled, sounding doubtful...almost disappointed.

Only he knew the answer why. Because there wouldn't be any wedding. Therefore, no kiss. No magic. No honeymoon.

Damn.

"Good save," Brooke said after they'd dropped Eliza and her chauffeur-driven Bentley back at the estate.

"For what?" Matt leaned against the side of her car.

They stood in the circular drive of his grandmother's estate, toe-to-toe, pretending to say goodbye as two lovers might. Just in case Eliza was watching from an upstairs window.

At least, that was Brooke's excuse for not moving away from Matt. For not looking away. For not getting in her car as quickly as possible and leaving.

Sunlight glimmered in his hair, turning a few blond strands in the darker brown waves to gold. His blue eyes, however, were dark, unreadable, impenetrable as a moonless night. Brooke's nerves flared with the heat from his nearness.

Why had she started this discussion? She should have said goodbye and left. But they had unresolved business. They had to figure a way out of this engagement.

"The bit about saving a kiss for the wedding," she added. "It was a nice save."

He gave a slight shrug.

"Are you really a romantic?" she asked, curious as to his reasons. "Or were you desperate?" she prodded, needing an answer to the confounding question of why he hadn't kissed her more than she should.

"What do you mean?"

"Were you desperate to come up with a reason why you didn't want to kiss me." She refused to ask him outright why he hadn't taken advantage of the situation. She shouldn't want to know. But she did.

"Isn't desperation the mother of invention?"

So, she thought, her heart plummeting, she'd been right. His evasive answer irritated her. But her raw disappointment rankled her even more.

What was Matt Cutter to her? Nothing but a man with deep pockets who'd offered a million dollars to the orphanage. And she'd do well to remember that. Why didn't she simply end this charade, take his money and run?

The startling truth was she didn't want to say goodbye to Matt. Not yet, anyway. He meant more to her than a means to help an orphanage or a way to get her mother to quit matchmaking. Much more.

She thought about him far too much. Why, she was starting to act like an adolescent with her first crush!

In the middle of the day, her thoughts drifted toward him. Her dreams revolved around him. And his kisses! What was wrong with her?

Her analytical mind refused to accept the obvious answer. She was not falling for him. She was not interested in him. He simply intrigued her, that was all. He never acted like the jet-setting playboy she'd expected. He was sweet and kind to his grandmother. Considerate. Possibly even a romantic at heart.

But more than that, he was sexy and mysterious. He was an enigma, she decided, shrugging away the uncomfortable idea that she might be interested in him as anything more than an interesting study on the human psyche.

How much longer would this pretend engagement have to last? She'd be better off when it ended, so she could forget about Matt. But she knew deep down that she would never forget him, never forget his kisses or his warmth, tenderness and strength.

Leaning toward her, the back of his fingers brushing against her arm, he said, "I thought you didn't want me to kiss you. I was just adhering to *your* wishes."

"Oh." Of course. Dammit.

"Did you change your mind?" he asked, his eyes glittering with mischief. Or was it need? The same need coursing through her?

"Change my mind?" she repeated, dazed by his touch, his nearness, by the raw urge to wrap her arms around his neck and kiss him.

"About kissing me." His mouth curled into a provocative grin. "You want me to kiss you now, don't you?"

She gave herself a mental slap. "What? N-no!" She lowered her voice. "Of course not."

She forced herself to step away. Jerking open the car door, she slipped into the hot exterior that seemed cool compared to the way he'd melted her insides like a chocolate bar in the blazing sun. "I have to go."

He chuckled. "Run, Doc, run. I promise to kiss you later. If that's what *you* want."

His smile faded as her car peeled out of the driveway. What had gotten into him? Why had he teased her? Why the hell was he punishing himself with this obsessive need to kiss her?

No woman had ever affected him this way before. And no woman would again. He simply had to get her out of his thoughts, out of his life. Which meant it was time to break off the engagement. Quick, before it was too late.

Over the next week he stewed about the situation. He'd spoken with his grandmother's doctor, who seemed as baffled as everyone over her quick recovery and sudden resilience. The doctor couldn't guarantee she wouldn't have a relapse. Her condition was fragile. Often sick folks rallied, the doctor had explained, before their health plummeted, before they— Matt's muscles tensed with worry.

What was he going to do? he wondered, propping his feet on his desk and sipping his morning coffee. He'd started coming into his office earlier than usual. Here it was quiet. Here he could escape his crazy dreams that always seemed to focus on Brooke, on kissing Brooke, on making love to Brooke. Here he could concentrate.

He couldn't marry Brooke. And he couldn't send her packing, either. So what now?

He certainly couldn't keep avoiding her. He hadn't spoken to her since the day they'd driven to the mission. Brooke hadn't called him, either. She was probably hoping he'd forget about her. Not a chance!

But his grandmother had been hounding him, telling him they needed to meet with the caterer, the florist, the photographer. This ruse was starting to cost him a small fortune. But if it made his grandmother happy, then it was worth every penny and ounce of angst.

The clipped tones of his secretary's heels against the hardwood floors echoed down the hallway. His gaze flicked toward the brass clock on his desk. The office was starting to stir. He needed to shift gears toward work. But his brain felt out of focus.

"This has got to stop." Brooke's voice startled him.

His heart gave a leap at the sight of her, but he decided it was surprise not excitement over Brooke's sudden appearance in his office. He certainly hadn't missed her during the last few days. And the way her turquoise suit flowed over her soft curves didn't affect him in the least. "What are you talking about?"

She slapped a newspaper on his desk, then another and another. The headlines grabbed his attention, as did the black-and-white photos of him and Brooke almost kissing beside her car. Folding back the cover of one magazine, she showed him an article announcing their engagement.

"I take it you're not thrilled with the publicity."

Her scowl deepened, her lips thinned. He had an

irrational urge to kiss her, to soften her mouth, to erase her anger. Or would it exaggerate it?

"I want this to stop," she said, her voice rigid.

"We can't," he said, thinking of his grandmother and not the way the light caught the tiny freckles across the bridge of Brooke's nose. "Not yet."

"Look," she said, her eyes blazing, "I didn't agree to marry you. I only agreed to pretend. For a short while. And it's been long enough."

"Fine, then," he said. "Break up with me." He pushed away from his desk, stalking around it and challenging her. "Go ahead. Do it. Right now."

She blinked as if stunned by his forcefulness. "Now?"

"Isn't that what you want?"

"Yes. B-but shouldn't it be in front of others?"

"Why?" he challenged, beginning to suspect she had her own reasons for not disintegrating their agreement.

"I thought…I thought it would be better if there were witnesses. So it would seem more real."

He nodded. "Actually, I agree. I think my grandmother should be there. Then she can come to the same conclusion—that we shouldn't get married."

"Good, then it's decided." She lifted her chin. "When are we getting together with your grandmother next?"

"Saturday." He crossed his arms over his chest, refusing to contemplate that the chill down his spine had anything to do with Brooke. He was simply worried about his grandmother's response to the breakup. "She wants us to have an official engagement picture made."

"Fine, I'll see you then." She turned on her sensible heel and started toward the door.

But he stopped her with a hand on her arm, turning her back toward him. A spark of something electrical, something magnetic, something unsettling rippled between them. "What are we going to disagree about?"

"Everything. If I say I want a color portrait, you insist it be black-and-white. If I say hello, you say goodbye."

"If you want us to kiss, then I'll say we can't."

"And vice versa," she said.

His gaze settled on her tempting mouth. He knew he wouldn't refuse to kiss her again. What a mistake that had been! And he hoped there'd be another opportunity. Soon. Before their engagement ended on Saturday.

"When were you going to tell us?" Peggy asked, her eyes gleaming with excitement.

Felicia tapped a manicured nail against Brooke's Formica countertop.

Cornered, Brooke stared at her mother and best friend. They had been waiting on her porch when she'd arrived home from work. "I, uh, guess I was waiting for it to sink in. It doesn't seem real to me yet."

It isn't real!

"Then it's true what the papers said?" Felicia asked. For the first time that Brooke could remember her mother looked tense. Her lips were pressed tightly together, revealing the tiny lines around her mouth that she always tried to conceal. She looked as anxious as if she were waiting to hear a judge's pronouncement on a divorce settlement. "You're going to marry Matthew Cutter?"

"Well…"

Peggy rushed forward and hugged her. "I am so excited for you! Congratulations!"

"This is the most thrilling day of my life!" Felicia exclaimed, her latest wedding ring flashing as she clapped her hands together.

"Mine, too," Peggy stated, her eyes misty as she released Brooke from a stranglehold.

Guilt pricked Brooke's conscience. Oh, she'd have a lot of explaining to do if the truth was ever revealed. She wished they didn't have to know about the pretend engagement. She wished she could have chosen the right moment—when she was more prepared—to tell her mother of her fake plans. But she didn't have a choice now. This was her opportunity to make her mother quit matchmaking.

Peggy leaned over and hugged Brooke. "If it couldn't be me, then I'm delighted he chose you."

"Oh, Peg."

Her mother beamed with maternal pride. "I've been dreaming about your wedding since the day you were conceived. And now it's finally going to take place."

"Mother—" She refrained from rolling her eyes and tried to look excited about her future husband. Matt Cutter. Her body felt electrified all right. For all the wrong reasons. Oh, heavens!

Felicia touched Brooke's cheek. "You'll be a beautiful bride."

Shameful tears pressed against the backs of her eyes. She couldn't go through with this. It was one thing to fib to a total stranger, but it was a completely different scenario to lie to her own mother. "Mom—"

Patting her arm, Felicia paced along the counter in Brooke's kitchen. "There's no time to lose. The paper said the date is three weeks away. Is that right?"

She nodded, feeling strangely numb.

"What were you thinking?" Her mother reached for a pen and pad to start making her infamous lists. "It takes at least nine months to plan a proper wedding."

"Your last one only took a week," Brooke mumbled.

"That's because I know all the shortcuts and secrets. Your wedding will be the talk of the town...the country...the world! It will be the social event of the season. Everyone will be clamoring for an invitation."

Watching her mother shift into full gear, Brooke felt something inside her snap. Suddenly her guilt vanished.

Felicia rested her hand against her chest as if to still her palpitating heart. "Imagine my daughter marrying someone so famous, so rich! Why, all my friends will be beside themselves."

Now Brooke remembered why she'd agreed to be Matt's temporary fiancée. And the peace their breakup would bring her. But suddenly the prospect of their breakup made her insides shift uncomfortably.

"Where is your engagement ring?" Felicia demanded.

"I don't have one."

"What?" Her mother frowned so deeply that even her forehead, which had undergone numerous plastic surgeries puckered. "Don't tell me he can't afford one. You tell him…better yet I'll make an appointment with my jeweler—''

''Mother—''

''—to fit you with a proper ring.'' Felicia studied Brooke's hand. ''You need a marquis to emphasize your long fingers. At least five or six carats. And definitely an eternity band with at least a dozen one-carat diamonds encircling your finger.''

''We didn't want anything so extravagant,'' she said, irritated at her mother barging in where she wasn't invited.

''Nonsense. Every bride wants a sparkling diamond ring to show off.''

''Not a boulder,'' Brooke argued, wondering at the same time what it would feel like to wear Matt's ring.

''I'd rather have a shiny new husband,'' Peggy said under her breath.

''Exactly,'' Brooke agreed. But she didn't want a husband. Did she? She certainly didn't want Matt. ''Mother, we made a conscious decision not to spend a ton of money on a ring I wouldn't wear.''

Felicia stared at her as if she'd spoken in Swahili. ''Why wouldn't you wear your wedding ring?''

''I wouldn't wear…'' She sighed.

Why did she bother? Her mother had never understood her. But Matt had. He hadn't argued with her. Fact was, it had saved him a boatload of money. But she sensed that wasn't the issue with him. He wasn't extravagant or flamboyant. She had a feeling he wouldn't want a fancy wedding band, either, just something unpretentious.

''I'll take this up with your fiancé.'' Felicia waved her hand as if dismissing her daughter's feelings. ''Have you decided on a location for the wedding?''

Play The Lucky Hearts Game

and get...
FREE BOOKS & a FREE GIFT...
YOURS to KEEP!

yes! I have scratched off the silver card. Please send me my **2 FREE BOOKS** and **FREE MYSTERY GIFT**. I understand that I am under no obligation to purchase any books as explained on the back of this card.

Scratch Here! then look below to see what your cards get you...

315 SDL C6KD

215 SDL C6J7

NAME (PLEASE PRINT CLEARLY)

ADDRESS

APT.#   CITY

STATE/PROV.   ZIP/POSTAL CODE

Twenty-one gets you **2 FREE BOOKS** and a **FREE MYSTERY GIFT!**

Twenty gets you **2 FREE BOOKS!**

Nineteen gets you **1 FREE BOOK!**

TRY AGAIN!

Offer limited to one per household and not valid to current Silhouette Romance® subscribers. All orders subject to approval.

Visit us online at www.eHarlequin.com

The Silhouette Reader Service™ — Here's how it works:

Accepting your 2 free books and gift places you under no obligation to buy anything. You may keep the books and gift and return the shipping statement marked "cancel." If you do not cancel, about a month later we'll send you 6 additional novels and bill you just $2.90 each in the U.S., or $3.25 each in Canada, plus 25¢ shipping & handling per book and applicable taxes if any.* That's the complete price and — compared to cover prices of $3.50 each in the U.S. and $3.99 each in Canada — it's quite a bargain! You may cancel at any time, but if you choose to continue, every month we'll send you 6 more books, which you may either purchase at the discount price or return to us and cancel your subscription.

*Terms and prices subject to change without notice. Sales tax applicable in N.Y. Canadian residents will be charged applicable provincial taxes and GST.

If offer card is missing write to: Silhouette Reader Service, 3010 Walden Ave., P.O. Box 1867, Buffalo NY 14240-1867

BUSINESS REPLY MAIL
FIRST-CLASS MAIL   PERMIT NO. 717   BUFFALO, NY

POSTAGE WILL BE PAID BY ADDRESSEE

SILHOUETTE READER SERVICE
3010 WALDEN AVE
PO BOX 1867
BUFFALO NY 14240-9952

NO POSTAGE
NECESSARY
IF MAILED
IN THE
UNITED STATES

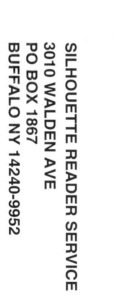

Brooke nodded, suddenly taking great joy in bursting her mother's expectations. "Yes. And luckily it wasn't booked yet."

"Where is it?" Peggy asked, opening the refrigerator and grabbing a couple of diet sodas. She handed one to Brooke, but Felicia declined.

"We should be celebrating with champagne," Felicia complained.

Not when Brooke was the soft drink type. Champagne didn't suit her. Neither did a five-carat marquis diamond priced in the stratosphere.

Popping the tab on the soda can, she answered Peggy's question. "There's a quaint little mission…"

"What?" Felicia gasped. "Don't you want to get married in a gorgeous hotel? Or even a grand cathedral? We don't have to be limited to San Antonio. We could go to New York. Or Paris."

"Or Hawaii," Peggy suggested.

"Or Tanzania," Brooke joked.

But her mother didn't find humor in her recommendation. "Let's be serious, Brooke. We don't have time to waste. Imagine what we could do with the Waldorf Astoria."

"No."

"How about a beach wedding?" Peggy asked, still hoping for Hawaii.

"We like Texas," Brooke stated. "Matt's family has been here for several generations."

"Of course you're right," Felicia nodded. "That's a definite consideration. The press would make a mockery of the ceremony if you flew off to marry somewhere else."

"So we've chosen a place right here in San Antonio. Well, actually, just outside the city limits."

"You have?" Felicia and Peggy echoed each other, both trying to hide their disappointment.

"This place is perfect." A strange sensation rippled down her spine because she knew without a doubt that the chapel was perfect. But was the groom?

As if she'd been doused with a bucket of ice water, Brooke felt her limbs go numb, her heart frozen. What was wrong with her? She was getting caught up in all of these plans as if they were real! As if she and Matt were truly engaged!

"A dirty, old, broken-down mission," her mother complained, permanent lines beginning to form between her brows.

"Brooke," Peggy said, interrupting her disturbing thoughts and her mother's criticism. "Aren't you going to ask me to be a bridesmaid?"

"Uh, yes. Of course." She tried to sound enthusiastic, but she felt dazed. "Will you?"

"I thought you'd never ask!" Peggy hugged her again. "I guess you found your Prince Charming."

Not hardly. Okay, she had to admit Matt was as wealthy as a prince. And he could be charming at times. Sexy and definitely irritating. But he wasn't hers. And he wouldn't be hers.

Besides, Matt wasn't riding to her rescue. She was helping him. Getting her mother off her back was simply a by-product of their arrangement. And she needed to keep focused on that goal. And off Matt Cutter.

Chapter Seven

"I don't like your outfit." Matt greeted Brooke at the door without so much as a hello kiss. If they were going to break up then they might as well get to it.

Although he wished he could tell her how the burgundy silk dress, which brought out auburn highlights in her dark brown hair, suited her. He imagined she would taste exotic, like warm, sweet wine. He yearned to kiss her and run his hands over her smooth, sensual curves. He wanted to cup her—

"Yes, you do," Brooke contradicted him, effectively dousing his thoughts with a bucket of confusion.

They were supposed to disagree, but he couldn't follow her logic. "What?"

"Remember…yesterday?" She turned away from his grandmother and gave him a conspiratorial look that hinted he should agree with her.

But they'd agreed to disagree, to argue, to break

up! They hadn't seen or spoken to each other yesterday at all. What was she doing?

"No…" He dragged out the word, hoping for inspiration, hoping to figure out what the heck she was doing.

"Sure you do." She ran her hands down the skirt, molding the material to her thighs, making his gut clench. "I showed you this dress, and you said it was perfect. Besides it goes nicely with your muted-blue tie."

"Uh—" She had him there. Their outfits did work well together. *They* worked well together. Maybe too well.

Sparks definitely ignited when they kissed. And they agreed instead of disagreed. But that didn't mean anything. It simply meant that they weren't following the plan.

"We don't have time to find something else for her to wear," Eliza Cutter snapped. "The photographer is waiting. This way!" She led them into her favorite room—the library.

Matt could still detect the scent of his grandfather's pipe tobacco lingering in the air, even though he'd been gone for more than a year. Lincoln Cutter had spent many evenings in this very room. Now his grandmother kept it as her dear husband had liked it. She could often be found here, remembering, reliving memories.

"What are you doing?" Matt asked, his voice barely above a whisper.

Brooke looped her arm through his. "Having our picture taken for the official engagement photograph."

He didn't buy it. Something was up.

Frowning, he pulled her closer and caught a whiff of an exotic fragrance lingering on her skin. He had a sudden urge to nuzzle her neck. "I didn't see your dress yesterday or—"

"Matt," his grandmother interrupted their whispering, "sit here in your grandfather's leather chair. And, Brooke, dear, why don't you sit on the arm?"

The photographer stood between anchored lights, his head bent as he fiddled with his camera. Matt assumed that the guy who was adjusting the lights to shine right in his eyes, blinding him momentarily, was the photographer's assistant. He refrained from complaining about the heat, the brightness or the way his pretend fiancée was snuggling against his side, making him hot and bothered. He tugged on his collar, which seemed to have shrunk around his neck like a noose. This was his grandmother's show, and he wouldn't spoil it.

"Philip," Eliza said, drawing the photographer's attention. "This is my grandson, Matt, and his fiancée, Brooke."

Setting his camera on a stand, he walked toward them in a lanky, disjointed fashion like a runway model. "Congratulations on your impending nuptials."

Matt gave the man a brief nod.

"This shouldn't take long at all," Philip said, "with such a beautiful subject."

Irritation nettled Matt, and he settled his hand against Brooke's waist.

"Thank you," Brooke replied, her cheeks turning a dusky hue.

"You know," Philip said, his gaze darting between them. "I have a theory about love."

Oh, brother! Matt gave a tolerant if not forced smile. Brooke's spine stiffened against the curve of his arm.

"Oh, do share!" Eliza turned her gaze on Matt and Brooke as if searching for a clue...or maybe confirmation that they were a perfectly matched pair.

"I believe people who fall in love have similar features. As if they're looking in a mirror."

Matt frowned. "That's—"

Brooke elbowed him. "Interesting."

That wasn't his thought at all. *Absurd* was more like it. But it didn't matter. Not as long as Eliza and everyone else thought they were right for each other.

Eliza nodded, her sharp gaze following the lines of their faces. "Hmm."

"See the shape of their jaws," Philip drew a line in the air.

"Ah, yes," Eliza smiled. "Stubborn, just like his grandfather."

Matt shifted in his grandfather's chair, the leather squeaking beneath him. He felt like a prize bull being put up for auction. "Let's get on with this."

"And the sharp angle of their noses."

"And their brows," Eliza added, obviously convinced theirs was a match made in a genetic lab. "Of course!"

"They will make a spectacular photo." Philip took another step forward.

"And a wonderful married couple," Eliza agreed. "You'll have many, many years together. Just like Linc and I."

Her prediction made Matt restless. He wasn't ready for marriage. Especially to Brooke. She was exasperating! Not appealing. But he knew he was lying to himself. She was intriguing, tempting and challenging. Exasperating was the right word after all. But he refused to acknowledge that his reaction to her was what actually exasperated him.

"Now, Matt, pull your beloved a bit closer," Philip said.

"Maybe she should sit on my lap," he muttered, already feeling uncomfortable with Brooke so close with her curves pressed into him.

"Hmm." Philip tapped his finger against his pursed lips. "What do you think, Eliza?"

"Are you comfortable with that, Brooke?" Eliza gave her the opportunity Matt had been waiting for.

It was a chance to dissent, to begin an argument with him, to begin the downward spiral that would wreak havoc on their relationship. Turning an expectant smile on her, he waited.

She grinned. "Fine with me."

No, no, no! That wasn't the right answer.

She slipped onto his lap.

A jolt of electricity sizzled through his veins. "What are you doing?"

"Enjoying my fiancé." She looped her arm around his shoulders for a brief hug.

He distinctly felt her bottom mold to the tops of his thighs. His blood ran hot. His abdomen tightened with need as her breast pressed against his arm.

"Now, lay your hand across her knee." Philip reached to position Matt's arm but he pulled away with a jerk.

He didn't need any help touching his fiancée. But actually he did. He needed help out of this sticky situation before he embarrassed himself with his automatic physical reaction to Brooke.

"Isn't this better than trying on tuxes?" Philip asked.

It was torture. Pure hell.

And he was enjoying it way too much.

"Brooke, darling, cross your ankles. No, the other way. There! And drape your hand over Matt's shoulder. Perfect. We want to show off your..." Philip frowned.

"There isn't an engagement ring," Eliza explained, her features creasing with disapproval.

"No, but there will be soon." Brooke patted his shoulder. "Right, honey?"

Honey? His nerves snapped like a flag in a stiff breeze. What was she up to?

"We're going shopping this afternoon," she continued.

"We are?" Determined to get this situation under control, he gave himself a mental shake. "We can't."

"Why?"

"I have to work."

"Nonsense," Eliza said. "Nothing is more important than your wedding. And buying a ring for your beloved...well, you should have already taken the time," she chastised. Just as quickly she changed her frown into a smile as she turned her attention to Brooke. "Now, dear, where were you thinking of going?"

"Actually, my mother wanted us to visit her jeweler."

"*Her* jeweler?" Matt asked. "She has her own personal jeweler?"

"You can't get married a dozen times without getting to know the person supplying you with diamonds,'' Brooke said as if it were a common, everyday occurrence.

Why did he think this was going to cost him? And not just in the wallet.

Philip tilted Brooke's chin toward Matt then stepped back. ''I want to see in your eyes how much you love each other.''

Love? Matt contained a snort of derision. He didn't even trust this woman who'd conveniently turned the tables on him. What the hell was she up to?

''That's it! Now hold it. Freeze!''

Wrong word, Matt thought, his nerve endings blazing.

The assistant handed Philip his camera. ''Perfect,'' he said backing away, adjusting the lens. ''I can feel the sparks. Now give me a smile that says you are in love!''

When Brooke's mouth lifted at the corners in a secretive smile, he felt shaken, unnerved, frustrated and something akin to pain. Definitely not love. How could one smile turn him inside out, make his skin feel raw, chafed? What was wrong with him? With her? *Get a grip, Cutter!*

''Matt!'' Eliza barked. ''You look irritated…angry, not like a groom in love.''

He was angry. At Brooke. At himself. At this whole charade.

Brooke touched the tips of her fingers to his jaw, making his skin tingle. ''What's wrong, darling?''

Darling? She was really getting into character now. What had changed? Was she suddenly wanting to keep his engagement ring…keep him? That unsettled him. *Forget it!* He wasn't in the market for love.

''Nothing's wrong. Let's just get this over with.''

She faced the camera again and flashed a brilliant smile. "Fine."

After a dozen clicks of the shutter, Philip looked over his camera at them. "Now let's have a kiss. A real kiss. One that'll burn up the lens."

Here was his cue! He knew for sure Brooke would argue against this. He had a ridiculous urge to tease her, push her to her limits, the way she'd pushed his buttons. With a squeeze of her waist, he met her startled gaze and dipped his voice to a low, seductive level. "Go ahead, darlin', kiss me."

"Of course, my love." Then her mouth covered his.

It was a good thing he was sitting down for this one. The shock might have made him collapse right onto the floor. He didn't have time to wonder what she was doing. Or why she wasn't arguing with him. Or why the hell she was kissing him like a lover would.

But he was enjoying it. Too much!

"Thank you, Philip," Matt managed as he saw the photographer and his assistant to the front door.

Brooke stood beside him, her arm looped through his, pretending to be the quintessential fiancée. His body felt as tight and unyielding as the stock market. He had to get his reactions to her under control. He had to get this situation in order. Beginning with what the heck Brooke was thinking. Why was she going against their agreement?

"My pleasure," Philip said with a toodle-oo wave. "I should have the proofs ready in a few days."

"Please hurry," Eliza called after him. "We haven't much time before the wedding."

Matt could almost hear the clock ticking in his head, counting down to his execution...er, wedding. He felt as if he were dragging his feet, delaying the inevitable, when he should be moving full steam ahead toward their breakup. He wasn't about to say "I do." And Brooke wasn't, either. Or was she?

She'd tangled his nerves into knots. With a look she could turn him inside out. With a simple kiss she could make him question his sanity. Maybe they shouldn't break up. Maybe they should...

What? What was he thinking? Maybe he should see Brooke *professionally*. Obviously, he'd gone loco.

A dark-brown delivery truck pulled into the driveway and distracted Matt from his uncomfortable thoughts. A young man retrieved a ruby-red rose out of the back and jogged up to the door.

"Delivery for a—" he looked at the card "—Mrs. Eliza Cutter."

"Thank you," his grandmother said, her voice breaking. She took the crystal vase and sniffed at the velvety petals. A white satin ribbon had been tied around the stem. Her shoulders drooped as she turned toward the stairs. "I'm a bit tired, so I think I'll go lie down for a while."

"Are you all right?" Matt asked, concern tightening his chest.

"Of course. Just old and tired."

"Maybe I should help you upstairs," Matt said, reaching for her elbow.

"I'm fine." She waved him off. "Stay with your fiancée. I'm sure you two lovebirds would like some privacy."

Wrong. No, right. He welcomed an opportunity to talk to Brooke. Alone.

But he had to do something before they talked, before he discovered her reasons for turning the tables on him.

As soon as his grandmother had retired to her room and he was left alone with Brooke in the great hall, he pulled her full against him. Her eyes opened wide. His body strained with an irrational need. His thoughts shuffled.

"What are you—"

"I could ask the same thing." But he wasn't going to. Not yet.

He took possession of her mouth. Her mouth popped open from shock, and her hands pressed against his chest. He kissed her the way he'd wanted to all along. This wasn't to prove they were "in love." It wasn't to impress anybody watching. It was strictly between him and Brooke.

It was something *he* needed.

Something he couldn't explain.

Something that would linger with him forever.

He wouldn't blame her if she slapped him. Or worse. Maybe he deserved it. But whatever his punishment, he knew it was well worth it.

Never had he tasted a mouth so soft and sweet. Her lips turned pliable, accepting. Her hands fisted the front of his shirt, instead of pushing him away as he'd anticipated, she pulled him closer.

The kiss turned hot, urgent, fierce. She wrapped her arms around his neck and pressed her body into his, her curves flattening to match the planes of his chest. He felt every arch and dip, every line, every degree of heat that throbbed between them.

An internal fire consumed him, fogging his brain, melting his resistance. His will began to crumble. He had to stop this insanity. Knowing he couldn't withstand any more without taking her right here on the marble entryway, he ended the kiss and stepped away from her.

"What the hell were *you* doing?" he asked, turning his frustration to anger.

She blinked. Her coppery gaze cut him like a rusty blade. "What?" Her hands fell listlessly to her sides. "I was kissing you. What were you doing?"

"I meant earlier. During the photo shoot. Why'd you kiss me then?"

"Why'd you kiss me now?"

He couldn't answer her question. Confused by his raw need to be near her, he focused on his anger. "We agreed to disagree on everything. But you were suddenly very agreeable. Why?"

She gave a slight shrug. "I don't know what you mean."

"The hell you don't."

She shot him a warning look. "Someone might hear us."

"Good. Isn't that what's supposed to happen? Aren't we supposed to argue...break up? Remember?" He crossed his arms over his chest, trying to contain his rancor. He wasn't sure which irritated him more—that Brooke hadn't broken up with him or that she'd kissed him.

Or that she'd stopped.

"Did you conveniently forget the discussion we had in my office earlier in the week? You were the one insisting we break up, remember?"

"What about your grandmother?" She leaned toward him. "She might be watching us this very minute."

"She's not an eavesdropper. Besides, she thinks we're...you know..."

"What?"

"You know." And he knew. But he didn't want to think about it. Because his dreams of making love to Brooke were vivid enough without him savoring the image.

"Kissing?" she queried.

"Something like that." He wondered if she'd contemplated making love with him. If she thought about him the way he thought about her. If her body craved his.

Shaking loose his thoughts, he focused on their plan. On the plan she'd changed without notice. "I gave you plenty of opportunities during the shoot to argue with me, to start something."

"I changed my mind."

His skin tightened with anticipation...no, irritation. He should have known this wouldn't work. If he'd asked one of the women he'd dated in the past for a temporary engagement, they would have tried to hold on to him, too. But Brooke's ploy surprised him. He'd really believed she wasn't interested in him or his money. He'd been wrong.

"Why?" he demanded.

She lifted her chin a notch. "We can't break up."

"Have you lost your mind?"

She gave him a sultry smile that turned his temperature up at least five degrees. "Not yet."

"Our plan was—"

"I know. But this charade is supposed to benefit me, too."

Ah, here we go! She probably wanted more money

donated somewhere. Maybe to her own bank account. His jaw clenched. "So, what is it that you want?"

"Peace."

He frowned. From him? "Go on."

"My mother is supposed to believe her only daughter is about to get married. When we break up, she needs to believe that I'm devastated."

"Can't you pretend?"

"Yes, but I need her to fall in love with you, too."

That stopped him. Could Brooke be in love with him? Was that what this was all about? No, of course not. She wasn't in love with him any more than he was in love with her. "Excuse me?"

"She needs to love the idea of having you for a son-in-law. That way she'll give up trying to match me with one of her country club chum's sons. After she meets you, no one else will live up to her standards."

He grinned. "You flatter me."

"I don't mean to." Her words socked him like a punch to his solar plexus with disappointment.

"Ouch. Keep on talking and our breakup will be a sure bet."

A tiny line appeared between her brows. "Look, you're charming and handsome, but there are a ton of men who meet that criteria."

"So what is it you're looking for in a husband?"

"My mother," she corrected. "I'm not looking for love or a husband."

"Okay. What's your mother looking for?"

"Money. And there aren't very many men who can compete at your level."

Money. It always came down to that, didn't it? "You're right."

For the first time he noticed the way Brooke's lip curled with disgust when she said money. His portfolio had always been an asset, never a liability. Why did it suddenly delight and irritate him? What was it about Brooke that turned him inside out and his world upside down?

"We need to razzle dazzle my mother with your wealth, make her think no one else can provide for me in the luxury and style that you can."

Incredulous, he ventured further. "And that's what's important for your mother? Not that her daughter's well loved?"

"She's always said you can love a rich man as easily as a poor one."

Something in her tone, in the depths of her coppery eyes told him what Brooke wanted...needed. Could it also be what he'd always dreamed of—unconditional love? "But you don't believe that, do you, Brooke?"

"I'm not sure I even believe in love." Hurt darkened her eyes to mahogany. "Or that love lasts."

He had a sudden, irrational urge to hold her, to erase her fears, to show her how deep and powerful love could be. He'd always believed in love. Watching his grandparents had taught him love was a rare and beautiful gift. Unfortunately, he hadn't yet experienced it for himself. But someday, somehow, he hoped he'd find the right woman.

Could that woman be Brooke?

The impulsive question startled him. He liked Brooke. But love?

"Your grandmother loved your grandfather, didn't she?" Brooke asked, her voice softening beneath the onslaught of hard emotions.

"Still does," he said, remembering how close the two had been before his grandfather's death. It was a love that far surpassed his own parents' superficial attachment to each other. Their love had always been about money.

"Did your grandfather love your grandmother?" On the surface it seemed a silly question, but he sensed a deep longing below the surface.

"Yes."

"How do you know?" she asked.

She sounded childlike. Her innocence touched him. He wanted to show Brooke about love. If only he understood it and trusted in it himself. His only experience and example had been his grandparents. "It was easy to detect in the way they acted."

She gave a slow, understanding nod. "It's easy to say the words. But not easy to live up to them."

"Actions reveal true feelings. My grandfather adored my grandmother. He treated her like a queen. Of course, he made sure she had everything she wanted or needed. But it was the little things that spoke of their love the loudest. Every Friday he gave her a single rose."

"Why?"

"To show he loved her. When they were just married and didn't have much money, he would pick a rose from their garden. The tradition stuck. Even after death."

She tilted her head. "You mean the flower that was delivered a while ago?"

He nodded. "My grandfather made an agreement with the florist that after his death a red rose would be delivered each Friday. But before his death, he didn't allow them to deliver the flowers. He stopped every Friday on his way home from the office and picked out the prettiest rose for his wife. And he always wrote a little note to her, telling her how much he loved her, what he appreciated about her, what he admired.

"She did little things for him, too. She always wrote him notes and stuck them in his briefcase or book that he was reading."

"That's sweet." Brooke's eyes glimmered with raw emotion. "And rare."

"I know. Someday I hope to do the same for my wife."

She tilted her head, watching him, studying him as if she could read his very soul. "So you do want to get married?"

He nodded, feeling a lump in his throat. He'd never thought much about marriage before this fake engagement, but now he realized there was something missing in his life. Something rare and precious—love. A certain someone who he could confide in, share things with, wake up with. "Someday. Don't you?"

"Not really."

"Is your mother the reason you don't believe in love?" he asked, intrigued and baffled by this beautiful woman and the deep wound in her heart.

"More my father."

"How so?"

She sighed heavily and slanted her gaze toward the stairs. "My mother...well, she is like a butterfly flitting from one rose to another, always looking for more pollen. Or money. But my father found what he wanted in my mother. He loved her so. But he was just a passing fancy for her. It devastated him when she left, taking me with her. I don't think he's ever fully recovered.''

"And you don't want to ever be that vulnerable, do you?''

Her shoulders squared. "No.''

"So, it's not that you don't believe in love. It's that you won't allow yourself to love.''

She met his gaze. "Exactly.''

Chapter Eight

Brooke's nerves felt chafed the following Monday as she walked into the orphanage, her no-nonsense briefcase at her side. Thoughts of Matt, their conversation about love, their kisses had rubbed her emotions raw. But mostly her admission about her father's heartbreak and Matt's insights into her reluctance to love had left her feeling unsettled...vulnerable. She'd tossed and turned most of the last two nights.

She hated to admit it, but they did have a relationship, funny as it seemed. She hadn't wanted to like Matt from the beginning. She'd set out to prove to herself he was a self-indulgent playboy. He'd stood for everything she'd resisted. Money. Prestige. Power. But she'd soon realized that the truth was something else entirely.

She hadn't wanted to feel anything for him. But she did. He made her think, made her question her beliefs, made her long for something wonderful and rare like what his grandparents had shared.

He made her want to believe in love. Which made her insides quake with fear.

After her mother's divorce from her father, Brooke had enjoyed little contact with him. Her father had turned inward, focusing on his loss instead of reaching out and staying close to his daughter. He'd said it hurt too much to see Felicia in Brooke's features, in her hands, in her smile. It brought him excruciating pain.

She'd yearned for that father-daughter bond and had hoped her mother's next husband would act as a father. But he hadn't. Neither had the others. So she'd stopped trying, stopped hoping, stopped believing. She'd closed her heart to the possibility of love—and she'd let go of her dreams.

Determined to banish Matt and the idea of love and marriage from her thoughts, she refocused on her work. She'd stayed up late last night trying to figure out a way to connect with Jeffrey, her withdrawn patient. As she entered the rec room where Jeffrey was usually waiting for her, she came to an abrupt halt.

"What are you doing here?" she asked, her irritation igniting.

Matt glanced over Jeffrey's head at her and grinned. That I-can-smile-my-way-out-of-this-one grin. She felt her heart give a tiny lurch in his direction but then she purposefully resisted, retreating like a catfish jerking away from a sharp hook eager to catch her.

Together, Matt and Jeffrey sat on a nubby rug, puzzle pieces scattered between them, a floppy-eared black dog lying nearby. They looked like two kids playing. Jeffrey seemed relaxed, focused on his task.

Matt looked charming, his hair tousled, his navy-blue eyes sparkling.

"We were waiting for you," he said, idly stroking the head of the Labrador retriever.

She stifled her irritation at Matt's intrusion. It wouldn't help *her* reach Jeffrey. But somehow Matt had accomplished a miracle all on his own.

Plastering on a smile, she walked toward them, her sensible heels clicking efficiently against the tiled floor. "Hi, Jeffrey."

He didn't look up, but turned a puzzle piece around, trying to fit it with another. The dog, however, stood and padded over to her, sniffing at her feet and ankles. The boy's gaze followed after the dog.

Patting the dog's head, she said, "Who are you?"

"Dodger," Matt answered. "He's mine."

"You have a dog?"

"You got something against dogs?" he asked.

Jeffrey looked up at her then, his brow furrowing with questions.

"No, not really. I like dogs. I just thought…"

"What?" Matt pressed. He watched his dog trot over to the window and stare through the glass at a bird who was searching the grass for a worm or seed.

Jeffrey traipsed after Dodger, his puzzle forgotten temporarily.

"I didn't think you were the type," she whispered low enough that Jeffrey couldn't hear.

"How come?" Matt asked, his penetrating gaze focused on her, making her uncomfortable. Why had she started this?

"I don't know." She shrugged. "You're always so…starched, so unrumpled."

He grinned. "Do you want to see me rumpled? Maybe in the morning?"

Her stomach made a slow roll as her world tipped precariously out of control. She refused to answer his absurd question. Irritation, and nothing else, made her heart pound. "What are you doing here?"

"He brought me a book," Jeffrey said, plopping down to resume working his puzzle.

"Oh?"

But neither man nor boy answered her silent question.

"How are you today, Jeffrey?" she asked, trying for a toehold in the conversation.

Matt shrugged as if baffled by the boy's silence. "I wanted to bring Jeffrey that book I promised him about cowboys." Matt touched a well-worn, well-loved children's book beside him. She could almost see him searching all those shelves in his grandparents' library until he found his favorite book from childhood.

She had an image of Matt as a little boy, hair tousled the way it was now, a lock falling innocently, endearingly over his brow, saying, "Read it again, Grandma." A warmth flooded her system, and she tried to shake the feeling, the intimacy, the mental picture.

"I thought I'd meet you here instead of at Bachendorf's," he continued, "so we could have a chance to talk. Before meeting with the jeweler and your mother."

"Oh." What did they need to discuss? How much money he didn't want to spend on an engagement ring? "I have a session with Jeffrey first."

"I found it, Matt!" The boy's gaze caught Brooke's, and his smile automatically faded.

Jealousy arced through her. Why couldn't she connect with Jeffrey? Why couldn't she help this little lost boy? Why did he have to like Matt? Why did *she?*

"You sure did, cowboy." Matt planted his cowboy boot against the rug and pushed against his knee to rise. "I have to go now so you can talk to Dr. Watson."

"Please stay." Brooke surprised herself. What was she saying? But what was wrong with Matt joining them this once? After all, he'd at least made a connection with her patient. Something she hadn't accomplished in six months. "You two look as if you're having so much fun."

"Sure," Matt said, "kick off your shoes and join us."

With a resigned shrug, she set her briefcase down and joined them on the rug. Sitting was not an easy task, though. She maneuvered her hips, shifting like a flopping fish, to find a comfortable position in her narrow skirt. Finally she settled, sticking her legs out in front of her, wishing she'd worn a fuller skirt or jeans even, something that would allow her to happily sit on the floor. Dodger sidled up next to her and rested his chin on her thigh.

"Here," Matt said, tugging off first one of her shoes, then the other.

She wiggled her toes self-consciously. Maybe she'd been too formal with Jeffrey. She should loosen up, be more casual.

"Isn't that better? More comfortable?"

Actually, it felt good with the cool air-conditioning

sifting through her hose to the bare skin beneath. But the memory of Matt touching her, caressing her foot, ignited a flame inside her. She snuffed out her reaction to him and tucked her feet beneath her bottom.

She should be more formal with Matt. Yes, that was it. No more kissing. No more foot massages. Why did that decision dishearten her?

"I hear there's a baseball game this afternoon, Jeffrey. Are you playing?" Matt asked, seeming to be more interested in connecting puzzle pieces than her at the moment.

The little boy studied the picture on the box, but his brow twitched with a frown. "No."

"How come?" Matt persisted.

Brooke decided to be silent, like a fly on the wall.

Jeffrey shrugged. "Nobody'll pick me."

"How come?" Matt asked.

"I'm not good at baseball. I always drop the ball."

"How are you at bat?"

"The same."

Matt handed Jeffrey a puzzle piece. "Maybe I can give you a few pointers."

"Wouldn't help."

"They used to call me the home-run king."

"Really?" Jeffrey looked up.

"Sure. I was even supposed to play for the Texas Rangers. But my grandfather needed help with the company."

Awe transformed the little boy's features.

Matt's revelation surprised Brooke. So he'd given up his baseball dreams to fulfill family obligations. And he hadn't complained about it. It was a simple, matter-of-fact statement. His family loyalty astounded her.

"Can you help me hit the ball?" Jeffrey asked, his voice tentative and restrained.

"You bet." Matt's gaze shifted to Brooke. The intensity in his blue eyes unnerved her. "What do you think, Doc? Can you field balls for us?"

"I don't know how."

"It's not difficult." Matt gave the boy a conspiratorial wink, as if saying, *Girls!*

"You might have to show me how. Or maybe Dodger, here," she stroked the dog's head, "could fetch for you."

"Let's go." Jeffrey jumped up and ran toward the door, Dodger padding along behind.

After putting on her shoes and helping to gather the equipment they needed, Brooke followed Jeffrey and Matt out back to the play yard. Dodger trotted off to sniff the periphery of the area. The orphanage had several acres with swings, slides, a soccer field and baseball diamond. Matt tossed Brooke a borrowed glove, then grabbed a bat to show Jeffrey the art of taking a swing.

The sun glinted off his almost-black hair, highlighting a few sun-tinted strands. The wind tunneled through the thick waves like a lover's fingers. Brooke had a sudden urge to smooth back a lock of hair tumbling across his forehead. But she refrained. And concentrated on her patient.

First, they played with an imaginary ball. Matt pitched a pretend ball several times and helped Jeffrey master how to grip the bat and take a swing. His patience and gentleness with the boy fascinated Brooke. She felt her attention slipping from her patient to her fiancé.

Pretend fiancé! Oh, yeah. Right.

"Are you really getting married?" Jeffrey asked, startling her back to reality. He was addressing her! Talking to her! The boy had never even acknowledged her. If being Matt's fiancée gave her extra points with the little boy, a connection that would allow her to help him, then she couldn't bungle this.

But how could she lie?

Suddenly the sun felt too warm, her suit too confining. "Well, uh…" She looked to Matt for help. "We, uh…"

"Yeah," Matt answered for her.

She shot him an irritated look. She hated lying. And she'd never lied to a patient. Until now. Well, technically Matt had.

"How come?" Jeffrey asked.

Matt's gaze collided with hers. Now what? Would they admit…er, *say* they loved each other?

"Well, uh, we…" Matt started and faltered, his gaze sparking something in Brooke that she couldn't fathom.

"I guess you love each other, huh?" Jeffrey tossed a ball into his mitt.

"Yeah," Matt said.

Love? Brooke wondered. There were feelings. Deeper feelings than she cared to acknowledge. But love? Ridiculous!

"Do you kiss?"

"Of course," Matt confessed too quickly for Brooke's comfort.

She refused to look at him and busied herself brushing dirt off her pumps.

"Do you—"

"Jeffrey," Matt said, a stern tone entering his voice, "a gentleman doesn't—"

"I was gonna ask if y'all wanted to have kids someday."

"Kids?" Brooke asked, dumbfounded. "Yes, I...um..." She couldn't imagine anything more wonderful than having children. "We do. Right?"

"Definitely," Matt agreed, too readily. Her skin prickled as she remembered his offer to get rumpled for her by morning. She could envision Matt playing catch with their son. No, no! With *his* son. Her heart thudded in her chest. What was she thinking?

"We definitely want kids." His bold look told her he was imagining a different scenario from playing catch. Her pulse raced. Then he cleared his throat. "Have you ever been to a wedding, Jeffrey?"

Relieved that he'd changed the topic, Brooke admired his ability to talk to a child. A lot of people couldn't. Too many talked down to them. Others made fun of them by asking silly questions like, "Have you ever been married?" Kids knew the difference. Kids knew who was genuine. Kids knew who to trust instinctively. And obviously, Jeffrey had made the right choice.

But could Brooke?

That sudden, irrational thought burrowed inside her. Why did she have to trust Matt? Why did it matter? Her fingers idly plucked at the leather string that bound the baseball glove together. For some odd reason it did matter if she could trust Matt or not. It mattered a lot.

She tried to act nonchalant even when she held her breath waiting to hear Jeffrey's answer, hoping to glean more information than a file would ever reveal. Yeah, that's why her heart was pummeling her chest. It had nothing to do with Matt. Or the way his shirt stretched over his broad shoulders as he threw another pretend ball toward Jeffrey.

"Once." The little boy's hands tightened around the end of the bat. He took a swing, pretending to hit the ball Matt had thrown. But he lost his balance, and the bat fell to the dirt. A cloud of dust surged upward, mushrooming around the little boy. He coughed.

"Here, try again!" Matt wound his arm and uncoiled his body for another pitch.

Jeffrey squinted, pretending to follow the path of the ball and then swung.

Matt clicked his tongue against his teeth, making the sound of a bat against ball. He looked up to the cloudless sky, following the arch that a ball would take. "It's outta here!"

"Really?" Jeffrey's eyes widened.

"Take a base." Matt cupped his hands around his mouth and made the sound of a crowd roaring its approval.

Jeffrey grinned and took off running, pumping his little arms with the effort.

Matt continued his commentary like he was a radio announcer calling the game into a microphone. "This might do it, folks! Jeffrey Dumas is rounding first. Bringing in one runner. And another. This could be it! The Rangers could win the series." Jeffrey rounded third. "And it is! It's a homer!"

Grinning all the way, Jeffrey ran toward home, little legs kicking up the red dirt behind him. Matt jogged toward him, greeting him at the plate with a high-five. He settled his arm on Jeffrey's shoulder. The two turned away from Brooke. She felt like an outsider, a voyeur.

"So, whose wedding?" Matt asked, retrieving a

real baseball he'd tossed toward the backstop when they'd first come outside.

Jeffrey breathed heavily, drawing in gulps of air. "My mom's."

Brooke knew Jeffrey's mom had remarried after divorcing his dad. Maybe that one tiny fact had garnered her attention, her empathy. How many times had Brooke experienced the same thing? But she hadn't been abandoned.

Matt nodded. "Must've been weird, huh?"

"Yeah." Jeffrey kicked the dirt with his sneaker.

"Okay, let's do it for real. Batter up." Matt took his position on the pitcher's mound and motioned for Brooke to move into the outfield.

"But…" She wanted to continue the conversation, press for answers, learn more about what was troubling the little boy.

"We need you in the outfield," Matt explained.

Patience, she could almost hear him saying. *Have patience with the boy. This is going to take time.*

But Jeffrey wasn't her biggest concern at the moment. She wondered how much time *they* had before the inevitable breakup. How much longer before Matt would say goodbye?

"Thank you." Brooke gripped the door, her nails digging into the soft leather of Matt's two-seater convertible. It reminded her of something James Bond would drive. Matt handled it with a deftness and sureness that made her imagine the way he would make love—thoroughly, carefully, thoughtfully. What was she thinking? The hot air blowing through her hair must have addled her brain.

"For what?" he asked, glancing in his rearview

mirror before switching lanes as he drove to the jeweler's to meet Brooke's mother and buy Brooke the biggest diamond ring this side of the Rio Grande.

Her stomach twisted into knots. "You really connected with Jeffrey."

"He's a good kid."

"Maybe I need to bring you along to all our sessions." What was she suggesting?

"If it'll help."

His answer surprised her. No false humility. No shrug and *It's no big deal*. No excuses like *I don't have time*.

"So, what did you want to talk to me about?" she asked, hoping she could find something, some reason why she shouldn't like Matt.

"Nothing. It was just an excuse."

"To see Jeffrey?" she asked, feeling a sudden, irrational surge of jealousy.

"Nope." His gaze slanted toward her, then settled back on the road ahead of them. "To see you."

"Oh." She trembled. Her heart slammed on the brakes. "Why?"

He shrugged. "Do you have to analyze everything?"

"Yes." She always had. But she refused to examine why her pulse skittered and stalled with each look from Matt, each touch and kiss. *It's better, Brooke, if you don't think about it...about him.*

"Well, don't." He maneuvered his car onto the freeway, accelerating, his hand shifting gears efficiently. "Not now. Not this time."

"Your mother is really something." Matt tossed the carefully folded sack holding the black velvet box with the ridiculously expensive engagement ring into his car.

"She's a piece of work, all right." Brooke headed around the front of his Mercedes.

It had surprised him that Brooke had gone right along with her mother, agreeing with her selection of rings—when he could tell she hadn't liked the selections at all. He admitted he hadn't known Brooke long, but he knew she had modest, unpretentious, elegant tastes. And her mother had been the exact opposite.

"I like her," he said, doubly surprised that the woman hadn't gotten on his nerves.

She paused, almost stumbling forward, then faced him again. "You do? Well, she adored you. But I was sure she was driving you crazy with all her questions."

"Perfectly natural for a woman to be concerned about the man who's about to marry her daughter. I'd expect your father to be worse."

"Yeah, well... My father probably won't make the wedding. I mean, *if* we were getting married. And we're not." There was an unsteadiness in her voice. "Remember?"

He grinned. "Officially we are. Until we do something."

But the something he was imagining was quite different from what Brooke wanted.

"Do something?" She frowned. "Like what?"

The something he was imagining made his blood simmer with need. Could she be thinking the same thing? Imagining them together? Legs entangled, lips meshed.

"Oh, right," she agreed, "the breakup. We need to figure out the best time."

Gritting his teeth, he nodded. "I can see why you'd want your mother to stop setting you up with eligible bachelors."

Actually, he wanted Felicia to stop, too! He didn't like the thought of Brooke going out with a rich playboy. Anyone other than him. And that made no sense. "She's nothing like you. I would imagine your tastes in men are very different."

What was he doing? Asking her if she could ever be interested in him?

"Polar extremes." Her answer deflated his ego. Did that mean that since Felicia approved of him as a son-in-law that Brooke automatically disapproved of him as her groom?

"Why won't—wouldn't—your father come to the wedding...if we were getting married?" he asked, trying to get his bearings after her almost blatant rejection.

"We don't see much of each other. Actually, I haven't spoken to him in a few years."

"Your choice?"

"His. He's never been as interested in me as he was in my mother. Said it broke his heart every time he was reminded of her leaving him."

Matt cursed.

Brooke's shocked expression made him apologize. "Sorry. But I hate that excuse. To me, he had a responsibility to you. And—"

"What about your parents?" she interrupted. "You never talk about them."

He shrugged, knowing he'd overstepped his bounds by coming down hard on her father. "They've always been too busy to be interested in me. My grandparents raised me. My mother and father were always traveling.''

"For business?"

"Pleasure. But I'm sure they'll come to the wedding. That is, if we were really getting married." He rolled his neck to release the sudden tension building inside him. "Why does your mother take marriage so lightly?"

"I don't think she does. Every time she marries, she's convinced 'this is it!'" Brooke sighed and touched the ornament on the hood of his car. "Her intentions are good, I suppose. She simply doesn't have the stamina for a long-term relationship."

Did Brooke? he wondered. "So what happens?"

"Somebody better always comes along. Somebody who's more handsome. More suave. More persuasive." She squinted against the bright sunlight, her nose wrinkling with disapproval, like a parent might after a child stayed out past curfew. "With a bigger fortune."

"Ah. It's the money, then." He flexed his neck to the side to stretch out the kinks from their afternoon of shopping for the perfect engagement ring.

He could have guessed Felicia's fondness for money and prestige. Felicia had known more about the quality of diamonds than he had. And she'd known more about her prospective son-in-law than the tabloids had ever printed. Obviously, she'd done her homework. He'd taken her barrage of questions in stride; his concerns centered on Brooke's reactions. But he hadn't been able to read her expressions.

"Was she moving up the matrimonial ladder?"

"So to speak."

"But you don't care about having a fortune?" he asked, his nerves pinched tight, not quite sure why her answer mattered so much. Worse, he felt vulnerable, as if he didn't have what it might take to attract Brooke. He crossed his arms over his chest. For some crazy reason he wanted to. Desperately.

"Money doesn't interest me."

"What does?"

"Helping others."

He frowned. She wasn't interested in a relationship. She'd told him that from the beginning. Then why, all of a sudden, was he?

"How did you end up being so different from your mother?"

She shrugged, rubbing her arms as if the sun had shrunk behind a cloud and the temperature had dropped ten degrees. Was the psychologist uncomfortable being on the proverbial shrink's couch? "It's not that uncommon."

"A woman not interested in money?" He laughed. "It is where I come from."

"Oh?"

He nodded, feeling a deep emptiness inside. He hadn't realized until just recently that he'd been looking for someone to fill that void in his life. Could that someone be Brooke? "Women I date are only interested in the size of my bank account, stock options and financial portfolio."

"I find that hard to believe."

He frowned. Obviously she hadn't met many of the women he'd dated. "What do you mean?"

"Money's not the only attraction you possess."

A ripple of pure pleasure circled through him. Her words surprised him. Not that he hadn't been told he was good-looking or had even his other virtues extolled, but he'd never thought Brooke had noticed.

"Really?" Now things were getting interesting. With a greedy smile he took a step toward her. "What else?"

Her gaze shifted sideways then settled back on him. But the toe of her left shoe turned inward as if she felt exposed. "You're a nice guy."

Nice? That was it? Not that *nice* was bad. But he wanted more. He wanted to know what else she'd noticed. He took another step forward. "I thought women liked rogues."

She reached out as if for balance and settled the pads of her fingers along the car's hood. "That's a myth."

"Perpetuated by whom?"

"Psychoanalysts who are looking for clients."

He laughed. "I see. Go on. What else do I have to offer a woman besides money and a congeniality award?"

"Well," she looked at the concrete parking lot, then at the sky, then over her shoulder as if to make sure they were still alone. She lifted one shoulder as if unaffected by him. But he knew better. He sensed it in his joints like a rain shower approaching. "You're obviously, uh, you know…handsome."

Her discomfort amused him. "Obviously? So *you* think I'm good-looking?"

She clasped her elbows, hugging herself, protecting herself. "What I think doesn't matter. All the magazines say you are. I guess they wouldn't put you on the cover if you didn't attract buyers."

"Uh-huh." He felt like a fisherman about to reel in a big catch. "What else?"

"Nothing. That's all."

He took another step, closing the gap between them until they stood only inches apart. "Do my kisses excite you?"

"Matt—" she cleared her throat "—I really should be, uh…" She glanced at her watch. "I have a—I need to get back."

"You didn't answer my question."

"Yes, well…"

"Then my kisses do excite you." He grinned.

"I didn't say that."

"You didn't have to. I remember how you responded each time I've kissed you."

"I did not!"

He slid a finger down her arm. "And then there was that kiss you initiated."

"I explained…"

He cupped her elbow. "Right."

Was she blushing or was the red tint that brightened her cheeks the effect of the setting sun?

She took a step away and drew a shaky breath. "We didn't decide when and how to break up."

He stared at her mouth for a long time, contemplating the pros and cons of whether or not to kiss her. The pros definitely outweighed the cons. Except for one nagging question— Why? Why did he want to kiss her? What would it mean? Where could it lead?

A part of him argued that it didn't have to mean anything. But he knew it would. It did. Nothing between them was casual. His attraction ran deep. So did his feelings.

And fear snapped him out of desire.

He let her back away, kept his hands to himself. "No, we didn't decide."

"I think we should break up in front of your grandmother and my mother."

That would be the best. It was time. Before he was in too deep. Before he really owned that ring he'd borrowed from his good friend at the jeweler's. "Okay."

"That way they'll both see the argument for themselves. We won't have to explain anything. Then it'll be over."

Over. Yes, that was best. "Right."

"Then you agree?"

"Sure. Why don't we take your mother and my grandmother out for dinner this Friday? And we'll let things progress."

But he wasn't sure how. Hell, he wasn't sure of anything anymore. Least of all his feelings toward Brooke. Or if he wanted them to break up. But he didn't know how he could stop it…. Or if he wanted to.

Chapter Nine

"Are you getting excited?"

Brooke glanced at Matt. An electrical current shocked her nerves, and her skin prickled in response. Abruptly she shifted her attention to his grandmother who sat opposite her at the private dining table the restaurant had provided.

Eliza waited for an answer to her question, her fork poised in front of her mouth with a bite of lettuce and tomato wedge on the end.

"About the wedding?" Brooke asked, feeling a tremble begin in the pit of her stomach.

"Of course, the wedding." Eliza rolled her eyes.

"What else?" Felicia added. The two older women looked at each other and smiled knowingly. "You're probably worried, too. All brides are. But it's a good sign that you two are so attracted to each other."

How would her mother know a good sign from a bad one? Her marriages had been based on lust and money. None of those had fared so well in the till-death-do-we-part department.

Maybe the attraction Brooke felt for Matt was a sign that it was all wrong between them. Yes, that's it! Such blatant sexual desire would destroy a relationship in the end. She ignored the analytical side of her brain that told her that was hogwash.

"So…" Eliza prompted. "Are you getting excited?"

"Oh, well…" She shrugged.

"*Nervous* might be a better word." Matt draped his arm over her shoulder. "Right, darlin'?"

"Right."

Wrong. Yes. No. She wanted to disagree with him, but her brain felt sluggish. Probably a lack of sleep—because she'd been thinking of Matt all night. And now she couldn't think straight with his arm around her, holding her close, calling her darlin'.

"Pish posh!" Eliza wrinkled her patrician nose. "There's nothing to be nervous about. All the details are taken care of. Nothing at all for you to worry about. Just sit back and enjoy the show."

Yeah, right.

"I'm sure the coordinator and caterer will handle things beautifully," Felicia said.

Brooke's brain shuffled to find something to argue with Matt over, a reason to break up. Dammit! Why'd they get along so well?

She slanted her eyes toward him. And why'd he have to look so damn good, no matter what he wore, whether it was a Stetson or a suit? She gave him a look that said, *Think of something! Do something! Get us out of this mess!*

He gave her a slight, understanding nod. Maybe she

should relax. He could handle it. After all, he didn't want to get married any more than she did.

"Maybe Brooke's nervous about getting married." Felicia sipped her wine, her maternal gaze narrowing on her daughter. "After all, marriage is a serious business. I'm always nervous before my weddings."

"That's comforting to know," Brooke mumbled.

Her mother lifted her brow. "Are you having doubts, Brooke?"

"Doubts?" This was her chance. Bless her mother! She'd handed her the perfect opportunity. "Well as a matter of—"

"Oh, dear!" Eliza sucked in a breath. She dropped her fork, her hand fluttering to her chest. Her skin paled, making the powdered blush on her cheeks stand out in stark contrast.

"Grandmother! Are you all right?" Matt reached across the table for her hand.

Eliza's lips thinned. "You're not having doubts, are you, Matt? Brooke?"

"We have been arguing quite a lot lately," Brooke confessed, determined to see this through. One of them had to be strong.

"No, we have not," Matt gave her a hard look, then turned a sympathetic smile on his grandmother. "Brooke's been a little hormonal lately."

"I have not!"

Felicia chuckled. "Arguments don't mean anything."

"You're sure, then, about getting married?" his grandmother asked.

"Yes," Matt stated without so much as an apologetic glance.

What was wrong with him? He had to know this

would be difficult for his grandmother. But they *had* to break up. They couldn't go through with a wedding just to keep his grandmother from having a coronary!

Besides, Eliza seemed to be recovering just fine. Her color had returned. Her hand steadied. Her appetite restored as she speared a cherry-red tomato. Brooke suspected her "illness" was all for show, all to manipulate Matt into matrimony.

"Arguments," Felicia continued as if nothing had happened, "just demonstrate that there's passion. And they almost always lead to making up." She winked. "That's one of the best parts of marriage."

Matt grinned and nuzzled Brooke's neck. His breath was hot; his lips gentle as they nibbled at her flesh. Her insides turned to mush. She tried to ignore the way he made her skin tingle and her heart rate accelerate. But she couldn't.

She squared her shoulders. This had to stop. Right now!

"That's right," he said, his voice deep and seductive. "There's nothing better than making up. Right, darlin'?"

"Matt…" Brooke warned, trying to lean away from him, but wanting to lean into him at the same time. Her conflicting emotions unsettled her stomach. What was wrong with her?

"Oh," Eliza fanned her face, "I'm not sure I could bear it if you two decided not to get married."

Brooke's gaze slammed into Matt's. *Oh, no! Don't back down now. This* has *to happen. We have got to break up!*

"Don't worry," Matt said in a calm voice that unraveled Brooke's nerves.

She nudged his foot. What was wrong with him? Why was he doing this?

He took her hand under the table and gave it a squeeze.

What did he mean? Did he want to go through with this ridiculous wedding? Or did he simply want to postpone the end? Her stomach knotted with confusion. And she realized she wasn't sure what she wanted, either.

To be dumped! Yes, that's what she wanted. Most definitely. Or did she?

"Well, I don't know about you…" she said, hoping inspiration would strike and she would figure a way out of this mess. Or maybe a bolt of lightning would zap her for continuing this lie. "…but—"

Matt leaned closer and kissed her on her cheek. "We've never been happier."

He wasn't helping at all! Especially not with her reaction to him escalating with each caress, each kiss. Irritation snapped inside her like an unfurled flag, and she dug her heel into his instep.

"Oh-h-h!" He shot her a pained look. "Oh," he said through gritted teeth, "we just can't wait to get married. We're excited, all right."

"Well, that's a relief." Eliza sighed and leaned back in her chair.

Brooke strangled the linen napkin in her lap as she tried to suppress her frustration, her irritation, her desire to smack Matt. Or better yet, stop his blathering on by kissing him!

No, no, no! That's not what she wanted.

Her stomach churned, as did her emotions, with confusion.

Then again, maybe she should kiss him. And really

kiss him! Maybe it would give him a taste…a bad taste of what it would be like to be engaged to her! Maybe then he'd leap at the next opportunity to dump her.

Pain radiated from Matt's foot where Brooke had tried to skewer him with her heel. What was he supposed to do? Give his grandmother a heart attack?

Maybe he should give Brooke a taste of her own medicine.

The meal dragged by, slowed by his desire to be alone with Brooke, to really touch her, to really kiss her. His gut contracted. Sweat dampened his forehead. What was wrong with him? He was acting as if he *wanted* to hold her—to hold on to her. Forever. Maybe he'd contracted food poisoning.

During the main course, when the ladies nibbled on their pasta and shrimp and Matt concentrated on his rib-eye, he tried to keep the touching between him and Brooke to a bare minimum. But it wasn't easy. His elbow grazed hers as he carved into his steak. His leg brushed hers. Accidentally, of course.

Thankfully, the meal ended.

Unfortunately, his grandmother wanted dessert.

After they'd ordered her a crème brûlée and the rest of them coffee, Eliza excused herself to the ladies' room. Matt was left at the table with an overeager mother-in-law-to-be and a reluctant bride. It was the perfect opportunity.

"Is everything really all right with you two?" Felicia asked, her voice lowered, her gaze shrewd.

Go for it, Cutter!

"To tell you the truth," Matt said, tripping into what he knew would be a fiery blaze with both doubt and concern tangled about his feet, "this engagement has been difficult."

"Of course it has." Felicia's brows slanted with concern. "That's what engagements are for, to test the mettle of your relationship."

"Well, it's being tested all right," Brooke agreed. *Perfect.*

He nodded. "I'm sure you'd agree, Felicia, that your daughter isn't easy to get along with."

"What!" Brooke shifted in her seat, her elbow jabbing him in the ribs. She glared at him. "I'm not the difficult one."

"Oh, I know," Felicia tapped her manicured nails on the linen-covered table. "She's always had a mind of her own. Never learned to play well with others."

"That's not true!"

Matt bit back a smile. This was going to be fun. "It's difficult to have a relationship when someone won't compromise. When it's always *her* way."

Brooke squared her shoulders, ready to defend herself. "Now wait just a minute—"

"You know it's true, darlin'." He read the fire in her eyes, the defensiveness. He had her right where he wanted her. Sort of. Actually, in his embrace would be better, but he wouldn't go there.

"I was perfectly happy for you to pick the ring of your choice," he said, suppressing the humor and his desire. "After all, I can afford anything your heart desires." He gave a wink to Felicia, who lapped up his words like a thirsty dog. "And even the honeymoon arrangements…I didn't mind that you insisted we cruise the Greek isles. Whatever makes you happy. I simply want to be with you."

Felicia sighed. "Oh, how romantic. The Greek isles! I went there on my fourth honeymoon."

Brooke rolled her eyes. Beneath the table her hand settled on his thigh. Her fingers were tense. His pulse jumped erratically.

"But," Felicia prompted, "what has been the final straw for you, Matt, sweetheart?"

He ducked his head, playing the part of the wounded fiancé. He rolled an abandoned spoon over on the table.

"It's okay," Felicia said, "you can tell us. It's better to air this in the open before it's too late. Before you feel trapped. I'm sure we can work it out."

In other words she was sure she could pressure her daughter into a compromise. Or a compromising situation?

He gave a heavy, exaggerated sigh. "Normally I wouldn't say anything. But I think it should be a mutual decision where we live after the honeymoon." He gave his mother-in-law-*not*-to-be a look that locked in her sympathy vote. "Don't you agree?"

"You're not thinking of moving out of San Antonio, are you?" Felicia asked.

"Not at all."

Brooke gave his leg a squeeze. He doubted she knew the impact she was having on him. His insides twitched with need.

Covering her hand with his, not sure if he could take any more pressure in a part of his anatomy that wasn't polite dinner conversation, he added, "Brooke wants to live in her apartment."

"What!" Felicia stared at her daughter. Her lip curled with disdain. "Why would you want to do that?"

"Well…" Brooke glanced at Matt. She looked unsure, unsteady. "I don't know. It just seems right."

"That's not what you told me," he said, knowing he was pushing her into a corner.

Her confusion turned to anger.

Matt stifled a chuckle. "You said you didn't want all the things I could afford. You wanted us to live like ordinary people. You wanted your salary to pay for our expenses."

Her jaw clenched. "Right. I'm comfortable living where I do. It's home."

"But," Felicia interceded, "it's time for you to build a home together. To take your place in society where you belong. I'm sure Matt would love to build you a great big house somewhere."

"I don't want a house, Mother. Think of all the upkeep."

Felicia waved her hand as if shooing away that concern. "Oh, there are people to handle things like that. I'm sure Matt wouldn't ask you to scrub the floors or mow the lawn."

"Mother—"

"Maybe you should see a marriage counselor. Or better yet, come visit my therapist," Felicia suggested.

"Mother, I'm a psychologist."

"A child psychologist," Felicia added. "Professional help might be good for you."

Leaning back, Matt watched Brooke fume.

"Hasn't done you any good so far," Brooke mumbled behind her napkin.

"I'm only trying to help, dear. Don't you want this relationship to work?"

"Uh, well..." Brooke's gaze slanted toward him. *Help!* she said with an imploring look.

You're on your own, baby! He crossed his arms over his chest. *See how you like disappointing someone you love.* "Well, do you want our marriage to work or not?"

He could almost hear her teeth grinding. "Yes," she said between gritted teeth, "of course I do."

"What were you thinking?" Brooke demanded.

"About?"

Brooke fisted her hands. "How can you act so casually about all of this?"

She matched him stride for stride as they walked down the River Walk. Her mother had suggested they take a "romantic stroll" after dinner to discuss their relationship, to find a happy compromise on their disagreements. Taking a stroll with Matt was the last thing Brooke wanted to do. But what could she say? No? Not in this lifetime.

Her stomach threatened upheaval at any moment. Nerves, she decided, a simple case of nervous jitters. She was, after all, a nervous bride-not-wanting-to-be!

It wasn't Matt. Or the way he affected her. She didn't want a man who made her want to strangle him one minute and kiss him the next.

Oh, dear! Her knees felt suddenly weak, almost buckling beneath her. She did want to kiss him. She did want him. Even a part of her—an insane, maniacal part—wanted to go through with this wedding. Maybe she did need therapy.

"We're supposed to get married. Soon!"

"One week from tonight to be exact." His tone

was casual, his demeanor relaxed. What was wrong with him?

Better yet, what was wrong with her?

She grabbed his arm and turned him toward her. They stood beneath a rock outcropping, the shadows shrouding them in privacy, the river rippling against the rocks. "What are you doing?"

"Nothing."

"Obviously." She narrowed her eyes, trying to read his thoughts, but his midnight-blue eyes were as mysterious and distant as the stars above them in the night sky.

He turned his gaze toward a couple nearby. The man leaned against a boulder. The woman stood between his thighs, her arms wrapped around his neck. They kissed endlessly. Longing welled up inside Brooke. She wanted that kind of passion. And she had it with Matt. But was it enough? They were opposites. *Puh-leese!* The last few weeks had proven the exact opposite of that statement. *Oh, dear, you have lost it!*

"What's that supposed to mean?" Matt asked, pulling her against him. Her nerves rocked with awareness. He jerked his head toward the kissing couple. "Is that what you want?"

"I, uh…"

Oh, yes!

Oh, no!

Say, no. Say it quick!

But it was too late. Matt tilted his head and captured her mouth, her breath and her heart. He drew her into his embrace as he inhaled her very essence. His kiss was deep, erotic, filled with emotions she couldn't diagnose or comprehend.

She should push him away. *Yes, that's right.* Her

hands inched up to his chest. But instead of shoving him away, they slid around his neck. Her fingers sifted through the fine hairs at the base of his neck. Her body thrummed with a need she couldn't deny.

She gave herself wholly to the kiss, to Matt. As their mouths fused, she felt their beating hearts closer...closer...closer in sync.

Then he released her. Stunned by the intensity of his kiss and her own voracious need, she gazed up at him, seeing tiny specks of light in his eyes. "You don't want to get married," she said, her voice trembling and shaking with uncertainty, "do you?"

She tried to ignore the anxiety churning in her soul. Did she want to go through with their wedding? It was crazy. She should be locked away for analysis for several months.

"Look," he said, his voice darkening to match the color of his eyes. "I know what you're thinking."

"I doubt it." She wrapped her arms around her, shivering from the realization that she cared very deeply for Matt. But that didn't mean she wanted him for a husband. They didn't know each other. They didn't have enough in common. They certainly didn't love each other.

Did they? Did he...could he love her?

It was an insane notion. She wasn't even sure she believed in love. Not the forever-and-ever after variety. Sure, there was lust, infatuation, obsession. But those all faded with time.

But a mutual love? Devotion? Fidelity that lasted a lifetime? Was it possible?

She doubted it. Wasn't it always one-sided? Didn't someone always end up hurting, aching from a shattered heart and broken vows? Well, it wouldn't be her.

"What did you expect me to do?" Matt asked.

"Excuse me?" She blinked confused by his question, by the sharpness in his tone.

"I know you were angry. But what did you want me to do? Give my grandmother a heart attack? Put her in the hospital again? Or worse?

"No, of course not." She knew why he'd reneged on their agreement to break up tonight. But it somehow didn't calm her nerves or keep her from wishing there was a secret reason for his reluctance. "Did you ever think that maybe she's faking it?"

"She's not. She has congestive heart failure. Major shocks are not good for her."

"So, what do you plan to do? Marry me? So your grandmother won't get a shock?" She couldn't keep her heart from pounding with dread…no, hope.

"No, I just—" He sighed and jammed his hands into his back pockets "—I thought we needed to take it slower."

"Slower! The wedding is next week. If we take it any slower we'll be sailing off to our honeymoon before we can say 'I don't.'" She squared her hands on her hips. "What was all that about a honeymoon in Greece and about my not being cooperative? I've been very cooperative through this whole thing."

He smiled enticingly, lifting one corner of his mouth, reminding Brooke how sensual and tempting his lips could be.

"I suppose we could break up in the middle of the wedding," she offered, her mind racing like her pulse.

"How?"

"We could have someone say they were in love

with one of us, that they'd slept with one of us the night before…anything.''

''That's one way to make national headlines.'' He scowled. ''Don't worry, I'll think of something.''

''What?''

''You didn't like my ad-libbing tonight?''

''No.''

''Good. You weren't supposed to.'' He turned on his boot heel and strode down the walk.

Moonlight glinted off the dark water. Matt rankled her darkening mood. But she wouldn't let him have the last word. She jogged to catch up with him and cursed the damn heels she'd worn this evening.

''So, what was all that about?'' she said, her voice breathy.

''I wanted you to understand what it felt like, to have someone you loved concerned and worried about our relationship. Now, you know.''

''Yeah, now I know.'' She knew a lot more, too.

It had bothered and amazed her that her mother had been so concerned. More than that, the whole argument had made her realize how much she wanted to please her mother.

Her whole life she'd bucked against her mother's scheming plans and high-brow ideals. But in her heart, Brooke knew that her mother loved her. And she loved her mother.

If—no, *when* she and Matt broke up, Matt had to dump *her*. Not vice versa. Otherwise, she'd be at fault. In her mother's eyes. And that wouldn't give her peace.

Her head started to pound. She'd probably be at fault, anyway. According to her mother. The light at the end of the marriage tunnel was fading. Suddenly Brooke felt lost, confused, claustrophobic. There was no way out of this mess. No way at all! If she didn't watch out, she just might have to marry Matt Cutter!

the sun and through the trees, and drilling at fifty feet deep, with heat shining in summer — and there is no vegetation this area. Not even a single sample could run this same table was empty and Cutter

Chapter Ten

Where once work had been a joy, now it was a safe haven, a place she could retreat to, where she could forget about Matt. Temporarily, that is, when he didn't show up at the orphanage.

Today Brooke had checked the parking lot when she'd arrived but hadn't seen his roadster. She'd expected to feel relieved, but disappointment had jabbed her. She was no longer irritated at her preoccupation with Matt Cutter, but frustrated and angry. Maybe even desperate.

She cared for him. Deeply. It might even be a slight case of love. Slight? All right, a full-blown case. But that only made her predicament and her prognosis worse. For how could she love him, when she knew he couldn't…wouldn't return her love? He'd told her more than once that he wasn't interested in marriage, in falling in love. He was scared to love. Just as she was.

She'd decided long ago never to put herself in her

father's situation and end up with a broken heart. But here she was, suffering mild aches, knowing that when Matt finally ended their relationship, her heart would crack wide open.

She shifted her briefcase into her left hand and opened the door to the orphanage. She expected the usual teeming noises of a TV tuned to some game show or sixties rerun, kids' laughter echoing through the hallways, the squeak of sneakers on linoleum. But all she heard was the hum of the air conditioner. Was something wrong? Had something happened?

When she found no one at the main desk, she turned the corner toward the rec room. "Hello?"

Then she saw Jeffrey. He sat on a table, his little legs swinging back and forth. His hair was rumpled, as usual. But today he looked different. He held his shoulders back, his head up. His eyes had a vibrant hue.

"Hi, Jeffrey." She walked toward him. "Where is everybody?"

He gave a slight shrug.

"Would you like to go into the rec room with me for a while?"

Instead of answering, he slid off the edge of the table. He might not be speaking directly to her, but he was more cooperative than he'd ever been with her. A part of her wished Matt had come today.

"You look excited," she said, walking beside him. "Is there something special happening today?"

Again he shrugged.

"Mrs. Morris told me a couple was planning on meeting you this Friday. Are you excited about that?"

This time his shrug was different. And there was a definite smile lurking around his pinched mouth. So that was it. He wanted a family. Who could blame him? She prayed it would work out this time.

"Why don't we work on a puzzle," she suggested, entering the rec room, "and you can tell me—"

"Surprise!"

The shriek of laughter stopped her cold. She turned and saw the other kids, most of whom she had counseled at one time or another, bounding toward her, tugging and jostling her. The teachers and care providers lined the rec room and clapped.

"What is this?" she asked, stunned.

"A party," Jeffrey whispered.

"Were you in on this?" She placed a hand on his shoulder.

He nodded. Then he actually smiled. Not a full-fledged, ear-reaching grin. But it was a smile that touched Brooke deep in her soul.

Then she saw Matt.

He stood along the back wall next to his grandmother, her mother and Peggy. Slowly he moved forward, walking toward her, making her pulse thrum. "Are you surprised?"

"I'd say. What's going on?"

Mrs. Morris, the director, bustled forward. "The children wanted to give you a wedding shower."

"A shower? But—"

Matt silenced her protest with a stern look. Then he wrapped an arm around her waist. "Wasn't that nice of them?"

"Yes, very."

He led her to a table decorated with balloons and presents. Her legs felt wooden. In the center was a white cake topped with an assorted bunch of sugary flowers. The children ran ahead of them, crowding each other, making enough noise to cause Brooke to wonder how they'd ever been quiet enough to surprise her.

"We can't let them do this," she said in an urgent whisper to Matt.

"Sure we can." He smiled and squeezed her waist.

His attitude nettled her. What was he thinking? These weren't rich patrons, people who had money to burn. These were children. They believed she was getting married. They expected a wedding! A wedding that would never be.

"Matt, we have to tell them. We can't let this continue."

"It'll be all right," he said, speaking low enough that no one else could hear. "I'll take care of everything."

He couldn't take care of this, any more than he could cure her broken heart. Some things even money couldn't fix.

Guilt washed over her. It was one thing for Matt to spend his money on this fake engagement and wedding that would never take place. It was another matter for the orphanage, with its tight budget, to spend money. On her. On a fake wedding. The children and workers at the orphanage had gone to so much trouble. For her! Tears pressed hot against the backs of her eyes. She couldn't let this charade continue.

"Congratulations," Mrs. Morris said, shushing the children with her arm gestures. "We are thrilled for both of you."

"Thank you," Matt said.

She ignored her wishful thinking that she was really marrying Matt. She kept her feet firmly rooted in reality. Not some fairy tale like Cinderella. "Mrs. Morris, I'm afraid—"

Matt pulled her close against her side as if that could silence her. Feeling his strength and the solidness of his chest against her clouded her thinking momentarily.

"The children did a couple of special projects so we could afford to get you a gift." Mrs. Morris picked up a silver paper-wrapped box. It had an overabundance of tape along the edges. The children must have helped wrap it.

"Be sure and save the bow," Felicia said, joining them at the table.

"What for?" Matt asked.

"It doesn't matter," Brooke said. "We can't accept this."

"You'd break the children's hearts if we didn't."

He was right. "But—"

"So what's the bow for?" he asked, lifting his voice and fingering the ribbon.

Brooke's mind spun out of control as she imagined him toying with a lock of her hair. A tempting shiver arced down her spine.

"You save all the bows from your prewedding packages," Felicia explained, "and make a bouquet with them for the rehearsal."

With a deft flick of his wrist, Matt removed the bow from the package and handed it to his mother-in-law-to-be.

"Matt..." Brooke breathed.

"And," Felicia continued, "every broken ribbon," she fingered the long curling end that had hugged the package tightly, the ribbon Matt had snapped in two, "means a baby." Her eyes shone. "A grandbaby. Oh, dear, I'm not sure I'm ready for that."

Neither was Brooke. As the children around them giggled, she felt her cheeks burn. She also felt Matt's steady, smiling gaze on her and refused to look at him.

He handed her the box and continued unwrapping the gift. The paper rattled, and her heart contracted. What were they doing?

"Don't worry—" his voice low and sensual "—we'll wait a while before taking that plunge."

Their gazes locked, and a shimmy of excitement rippled through her. She imagined Matt holding their baby, his eyes full of love, her life full and complete. Was that what she really wanted? A husband? A baby? A family?

"But what about the children." Her voice trembled. "I mean, the children here at the orphanage."

"They'll get their money back," he whispered as he leaned close to rip at one end of the package. "We'll reimburse them when we've made the announcement. They'll receive even more. Remember our agreement?"

How could she forget? Why did she keep forgetting? She needed her head…or her heart…examined.

Matt lifted the top off the box. The children craned their necks as if they didn't know what was inside. Brooke peered closer as Matt pulled the tissue paper out of the way. Then her breath caught in her chest.

"Oh, my!" she breathed. Her heart ached. Guilt pressed down on her. What had she done?

"Wow!" Matt pulled a quilt out of the box. It was pieced together with tiny crooked stitches. Each square had been lovingly sewn by a child's hands.

Some squares had wedding bells. Others had flowers and candles. Each had a child's name embroidered on it.

"How did you do this?" she asked, her heart filling with a surge of emotions.

"It wasn't easy," Mrs. Morris said, her hand resting against her heart with pride. "Some of the children thought sewing was sissy. But they all did their part. They even helped put it all together."

"It's beautiful." Brooke blinked back tears.

"This will be something you can cherish forever," Eliza said, fingering an edge of the quilt.

Forever. It was something that didn't apply with this wedding. Certainly not with Matt. But Brooke wished for the impossible.

They couldn't give this gift back to the children. They couldn't return it for a full refund. And she couldn't marry Matt just to please the children.

But would marrying Matt bring her a fulfillment she'd only dreamed about? Her head pounded with questions and uncertainty. What was she going to do now?

"You can now kiss your bride." The minister glanced up from his notes. His bushy gray brows arched toward his receding hairline.

Matt's stomach plummeted like a skydiver without a parachute. "Now?"

The minister shrugged. "It's the rehearsal. Go ahead and practice, if you want."

Matt didn't need any practice. Not with Brooke. Their kisses were already too intense, too unnerving, too…much.

"I do like to see an eager bridegroom," Felicia

whispered behind him, as she and the others, including his grandmother, watched from the pews behind them.

How eager was he supposed to be? Yes, he wanted to kiss Brooke. Actually he wanted to do more than kiss her. But he shouldn't. Oh, man, he shouldn't! Because he knew he might not be able to stop. And this insanity had to stop. Now.

"No kissing." Brooke placed a hand against his chest. Her eyes widened as if she had felt a jolt of awareness, too.

Could she feel his pulse pounding? Could she sense the longing in his heart? Part of him wanted to bolt out the door of the mission. He'd never run from anything in his life. No woman had ever scared him. But no woman had ever made him want to commit, either. Another part of him—a lunatic part—wanted to stay, to make this wedding real.

It's not real, Cutter. The feelings you're having are fake...imagined. Get that through your thick skull! This is not reality!

But he wanted it to be. He wanted Brooke as his bride with all the wedding trimmings and a honeymoon to top it off.

He'd never bucked the idea of marriage. He'd rebelled against marrying a bride who loved him only for his money. But Brooke was different. She didn't care about money.

But could she care about him? Could she love him?

He realized at that moment that he could love her. With the kind of love that wrapped around your heart and bound you to another for an eternity. The thought didn't scare him. It made him yearn for that closeness.

But what frightened him was that his feelings might

be confused because of Brooke's total disregard for money, for his lifestyle…for him?

"You don't want to kiss Matt?" Felicia asked, her voice rising in horror.

He knew better. He'd felt her respond. And he could sense her hesitation now.

Tempted to jump in and save her, he decided to wait, to let her answer her mother's question. Maybe it would clarify his feelings.

"I mean," she said, her voice faltering. "Uh…"

Her gaze remained magnetized to Matt's. Something sizzled between them, an awareness. No, it was more than that. An understanding.

She did want to kiss him. Just as he wanted to kiss her. But not now. Not here. Not in front of all these people. This time, she wanted it in private.

"Um, not now." She let her hand fall to her side and stepped away from Matt. "Not in front of all these people."

"A shy bride," Eliza muttered, "how rare these days. And totally refreshing. But you'll have to get ready for tomorrow," she added. "Your guests will expect a kiss right out of the storybooks."

The minister cleared his throat and slipped his notes into his coat pocket. "Tomorrow, after the kiss, you'll turn toward the congregation."

With a hand on Brooke's and Matt's shoulders, he urged them to face the rest of the wedding party and those who would be attending the rehearsal dinner later that evening.

With Brooke by his side, Matt suddenly realized they stood as stiff as a plastic bride and groom atop a wedding cake. What now? What should they do now? Run for their freedom?

Not a bad idea.

Until Brooke slipped her arm through his. He felt his body warm to new possibilities, his heart open wider. Maybe they should go ahead with this farce. Or maybe they could turn it into a real wedding.

"The matron of honor will hand back your bouquet," the wedding coordinator said, gesturing between mother and daughter.

Felicia handed Brooke a bouquet of white and pink bows that had been taken off the wedding presents from the surprise shower. "Then I'll fluff her veil."

"And I'll rearrange the train on her dress," Peggy said. "But don't worry I won't let you flash anybody."

"That's comforting," Brooke mumbled.

Straightening his tie, the minister continued, "When everyone is finished fussing over the bride, I'll announce you as Mr. and Mrs. Matthew Cutter."

Brooke's spine stiffened. She looked over her shoulder at the minister. "For your information, I'm a doctor."

"Oh," the minister gave Matt a questioning look. "Mr. And Dr. Matthew Cutter? Doesn't quite have the same ring, does it?"

"Maybe just for tomorrow you could be Mrs.," Felicia offered.

"Forget all those years of school?" Brooke eyed her mother. "Forget all my patients? I don't think so. Besides, I won't be taking Matt's name."

Her statement seemed to suck all the air out of the room. Complete silence settled around them. Here we go, Matt thought. This should take care of everything. Once and for all. But he felt himself dragging his feet, unwilling to let Brooke go.

"You won't?" the minister asked, still staring at Matt, waiting for him to agree or disagree.

But he couldn't think of anything but Brooke, the way her hair shimmered in candlelight, the sparkle in her eyes, the curve of her mouth. And he wanted to kiss that mouth and go on kissing Brooke for a lifetime...or longer.

"That's unseemly," his grandmother stated.

"Brooke," Felicia said, trying to soothe the in-laws and reprimand her daughter at the same time, "how awful could it be to take your husband's name? It should be an honor."

"It should be, but all my degrees are in my name. I worked damn hard for them. I'm known professionally. Dammit, I like my name." Brooke crossed her arms over her chest. "Besides, professionally it wouldn't be wise to switch now."

"Nonsense," Matt heard himself say. Then he wished he'd considered before he spoke.

Her hold on his arm tightened. But was she encouraging him or discouraging him from beginning an argument that could potentially destroy their relationship. That's what he wanted, right?

Right.

Wrong.

Wrong? What was wrong with him?

Did he really want to fight about this? Because he knew what Brooke was doing. He knew she was taking sides, drawing the battle line between them. Frankly he didn't care if she kept her name or changed it to Alberta. Sure, it would be easier as a married couple if they had the same name but...

Wait a minute! They weren't getting married. He had to take the opposite side. Why was he making excuses? Because he didn't want their relationship to end over something so trivial.

Because he didn't want their relationship to end.

Brooke pulled away from him and lifted her chin defiantly. "Is this a problem for you? My keeping my own name?"

"No."

She pinched his arm.

"I mean, yes." Damn, what did he mean?

"You're sounding very chauvinistic."

Boy did he know it. And he'd suffer for it in the papers and magazine articles if this leaked. And it would.

But that wasn't the reason he was fumbling, trying to find a way to agree with her. When he should be disagreeing. The real reason made his pulse skitter to a halt.

"I was proud and honored to take my Linc's name." Eliza drew herself up to her full height of five feet even. "I would imagine any man would want his wife to take his. Matt, too. It's natural."

"No, it's not," Brooke said. "I've been Brooke Watson for my entire life. It's not natural to turn my back on everything I am and become someone else."

"But you're not turning your back on who you are. That won't change," Felicia added. "Matt, how do you really feel about this?"

"I don't know." Realizing he'd spoken about his feelings for Brooke more than the argument at hand, he jammed his hands in his pants pockets.

"Well, you decide," Brooke said. "Is it something you can live with or not?"

Could he live with Brooke? The real question was—could he live without her?

"I don't know," he repeated, his mind churning as his heart raced. "I don't like it." He didn't like the way she made him feel confused and muddled, hot and cold, angry and elated. Maybe he was coming down with the flu.

"You don't like what?" Brooke asked, staring at him intently, trying to read his thoughts.

This had to stop. Now, he decided. "A woman should take her husband's name. I always imagined my wife would be Mrs. Matt Cutter, not listed under a different letter of the alphabet in the phone book."

Eliza nodded. "It does make things difficult for those sending you Christmas cards or wedding invitations. How do you make out the envelope?"

"Oh, I agree!" Felicia said. "It fouls up everything."

Brooke rolled her eyes. "What does it matter? It's my decision."

"Our decision," he corrected. "I want to be a couple, not two people with separate lives. But it seems as if you'd rather go on being single."

"Being a couple doesn't mean we have to lose our own identities," she said.

Now we're rolling. Now is the time. Just say it, Cutter. Say this isn't going to work. But the words jammed and snagged on his raw needs and longings.

"Maybe you should discuss this in private," the minister suggested.

Brooke gave a terse nod. "Fine."

Matt swept his gaze over the small group gathered. "Could you give us a few minutes?"

Quickly most retrieved their belongings and filed out of the chapel. But his grandmother stayed behind. As did Brooke's mother. Oh, brother.

"Would you like me to call my therapist?" Felicia asked. "I'm sure he could help you reach a compromise. This is such a silly disagreement."

"No, Mother."

"See, Matt was right. You are being difficult. You don't want to compromise. It's your way or no way. Well, that's no way to run a marriage."

"And you should know. Right, Mother?"

Felicia's mouth thinned as she backed down the aisle.

"I know you two can work this out," Eliza stated, her voice warbling with suppressed concern. Slowly she turned and retreated, leaving them alone in the flickering candlelight.

"That was good," Brooke said, her eyes twinkling. "Very good. Now we can tell them that we couldn't reach an agreement. This was just one of a million things we couldn't agree on. So, we called off the wedding."

"Seems kind of silly."

"Who cares?"

"My grandmother. Your mother." *Me.*

Her mouth twisted. He had an urge to silence her with a kiss. "I meant, no one cares about the reason, whether it's silly or not."

"Sure they do. I do."

"Why are you being so difficult about this?" she asked.

He shrugged. "Fine. Who will we say called off the wedding? You?"

"Oh, no. You did."

He shook his head. "Not me. I can't explain that to my grandmother. You'll have to do it."

"I can't!"

Hope surged through him. Maybe, just maybe, she didn't want to, either.

"My mother will never understand why I broke up with the richest man in Texas. You have to dump me."

"That would break my grandmother's heart." *And mine.*

"You know, Matt, I'm beginning to think you don't want to—"

A buzzer interrupted her and saved Matt from having to explain something he couldn't understand himself.

"What's that?"

"My service." She punched a button on her beeper. "It's the orphanage. I've got to make a call."

He handed her his cell phone before she could descend the three steps to the pews where she'd left her purse. She punched in a sequence of numbers.

"This is Dr. Watson." She gave a somber nod, listening to the other person, then waited. "They're transferring me," she said to Matt. "Hello? Mrs. Morris? Yes, I received your message." She turned slightly from Matt. "What's happened?"

When she snapped the cell phone closed, she looked at Matt. A fierce emotion burned in her eyes. "It's an emergency. Will you give my apologies to everyone?"

"What's the matter?"

"It's Jeffrey." She grabbed her purse from the front pew and slung it over her shoulder. "He needs me."

"I'm coming with you."

Chapter Eleven

They made some quick apologies to the wedding party, and in less than thirty minutes Matt and Brooke pulled into the orphanage's parking lot. Red flashing lights lacerated the darkness and shredded Brooke's nerves. Opening the car door, she bolted past the fire engines, police cruisers and ambulance. It became an obstacle course to get past the children and workers who stood outside, clumped in tiny groups, their voices hushed with concern. Brooke pushed through the glass doors and entered the orphanage. The bright lights were harsh and unnatural at this time of night, making her squint.

She looked left, then right. When she spotted Mrs. Morris, she ran toward the director. "What's happened?"

"It's fine now." The older woman's gray hair was disheveled. "We should all stay calm."

Matt reached them then. "Where's Jeffrey?"

"He's being checked by a paramedic." Mrs. Morris jerked her chin toward the rec room. She looked like a mother hen who'd had her feathers ruffled.

"Is he hurt?" Brooke asked, her concern inching up another notch.

"He's fine. It's just a precaution. He took quite a tumble off the back fence."

"Off the fence?" Matt repeated. "It's at least ten feet tall."

The director nodded. She gripped her hands together, her knuckles white from the strain of the evening. "He's fine now."

"Can I talk to him?" Brooke asked.

"That's why I called you." Mrs. Morris shook her head. "I don't understand why he did this."

"He met with that couple today," Brooke explained to Matt.

"Yes, but they *wanted* to proceed." Mrs. Morris's brow folded into a fan of wrinkles.

"They did?" The news surprised Brooke. Not that she didn't think Jeffrey would make a terrific addition to any family. But she had figured the couple had turned him down and that the little boy was depressed.

"Yes, that's why I can't figure out why he would try to run away." Mrs. Morris pursed her lips. "I thought he wanted a family of his own. He clearly wasn't happy here. But now the couple may back out altogether. After they hear what happened tonight. Couples looking to adopt aren't interested in troublemakers."

"Jeffrey isn't a troublemaker." Brooke clenched her teeth. "He's a troubled little boy. And we're helping him."

Matt squeezed her hand. "Maybe he doesn't want *any* family. Maybe he wants *his*."

"Possibly." Brooke tapped a finger against her lips, contemplating the many possibilities. "But I guess the best person to ask is Jeffrey."

"I agree. Let's go." Matt laced his fingers with hers, giving her a calm sensation. Together they walked toward the rec room.

The television, which usually ran all day, every day, had been muted. Lucy Ricardo silently shoved chocolates into her mouth. But there was no one watching to laugh. A forsaken teddy bear lay on the center rug.

Brooke's mind churned with what could have happened. Jeffrey could have been hurt...or worse. Her heart pounded out the possibilities. But she couldn't think of them now. She had to figure out a way to keep anything like this from happening again.

Her gaze located Jeffrey sitting at a miniature table across the room. He held his arms crossed over his chest, his mouth drawn tight. The paramedic squatting next to him wrapped the portable blood pressure cuff around itself and stuck it in a plastic container. Slowly he stood, his gaze settling on Brooke and Matt.

"He's okay. Just a few scrapes and bruises." Bending to pick up his equipment, the paramedic said, "See ya, Jeffrey. You be more careful from now on."

Matt moved first toward the little boy. "Hey, cowboy."

Jeffrey glanced up.

"Mind if I sit with you for a bit?" he asked.

The little boy shrugged.

Brooke stepped closer and noticed the dark bruise

blossoming on the side of his face. "That's some shiner. Does it hurt?"

He gave a small, imperceptible nod.

"Would you like an ice pack?"

Jeffrey shook his head.

Brooke settled into the miniature seat opposite Matt, tilting her shoulders toward the little boy.

"You're tough, right, pardner?" Matt gave the boy a soft punch to his shoulder.

The boy eyed Matt for a moment. "How come you're here?"

The question surprised Brooke. There was no resentment in his tone, only astonishment. She waited for Matt to answer.

"I was worried about you," Matt said, "that's why. You gave us all a good scare."

"Why?"

"Because we care about you, Jeffrey," Brooke said.

He remained silent, but his fists were closed in denial.

"What was it like standing up on that fence post?" Matt asked. "It's a long way up there. Must've taken some guts to climb up that high."

"I was scared," Jeffrey admitted.

"I bet," Matt said, looking out the back windows to the play area and the fence Jeffrey had fallen from. "I sure would have been."

"You're not scared of nothin'," Jeffrey said.

"Sure I am."

"Like what?" Jeffrey challenged.

"Bees. I hate those stingers they have."

"Yeah," Jeffrey said, his brows drawing together in commiseration.

"Dentists," Brooke added. "I hate their drills."

Both Matt and the little boy nodded in agreement.

"And being alone," Matt said. Truth saturated his words, filling his voice with raw emotions.

Brooke watched him closely. This man always managed to surprise and intrigue her. She never would have thought, seeing his picture in tabloid magazines while she stood in line at the grocery store or heard about him on the news, that Matt Cutter could ever be lonely. Instinctively she knew it wasn't some line he was feeding the little boy. He was being honest. And yet his simple statement raised many questions in Brooke's mind.

Jeffrey looked at the bigger, stronger man. "You, too?"

"Uh-huh. I always hated being left alone as a kid."

"Did your folks leave you?"

"Not the same way yours left," Matt said, "but they left."

"How?" Jeffrey leaned forward, propping his elbows on the table.

"They traveled."

"Like on vacations?" Jeffrey asked.

"When they weren't gone on business trips."

"Yeah, but your folks were home for your birthday and Christmas." The scepticism in Jeffrey's voice tore at Brooke.

"Not always. And when they were, they made it clear they didn't want to be there. With me." The pain in Matt's eyes, the hurt in his voice spoke to Brooke's heart.

She'd always thought of him as a footloose and fancy-free playboy without a care in the world. But she could easily imagine him sitting in a window seat of his grandmother's estate, watching and waiting for his parents' return. Only to be rejected and made to feel like a nuisance.

"My folks didn't want me, either." Jeffrey twisted a shoestring around his finger. "My dad left my mom before I was born. And my mom dumped me here."

"Maybe she did want you, but she just couldn't care for you," Matt suggested.

"Nope. She told me I was too much trouble."

"Then she's an idiot." Matt's voice sharpened with conviction and condemnation.

Jeffrey's eyes widened, then he shrugged.

Silence ticked slowly between them until Brooke said, "That nice couple you visited with today want you."

"No, they don't." Jeffrey scraped the sole of his sneaker with his thumbnail. "They wanted their own baby, but she couldn't get pregnant. They only want a substitute. They don't really want me."

Her heart filled with sorrow for this little boy who so desperately needed to feel loved and wanted. She wished she could scoop him up in her arms and adopt him herself. She wished she could provide him with a family. But she didn't have one of her own. Not really.

The realization hit her broadside. That's what she'd wanted, what she'd always longed for—a normal, stable, loving, caring family. But she'd stifled that desire, locked it away in a dark corner of her soul.

Maybe that's why she felt drawn to Matt. He was more normal than she'd ever imagined before she met him. His feet were firmly grounded in reality and the knowledge that nothing was more important than family. He was obviously capable of loving someone deeply, completely. He was loyal and tender. If Prince Charming existed, then he wore a Stetson and lived in San Antonio.

No wonder she didn't want to end their engagement. No wonder she wanted to go through with the wedding. But she wondered if he could ever love her. That one question kept her from falling in love with him.

But she knew it was already too late. She couldn't stop herself, any more than she could erase the need to kiss him, the longing to be near him, the craving to be a part of his life. Because she already loved him.

And it could only end one way—with her heart shattered.

What are you afraid of? Jeffrey's question had skewered Matt right through the heart. During the three hours they'd talked and played in the rec room, trying to understand Jeffrey's troubles, Matt had asked himself the same question over and over. *What are you afraid of?*

It was more than being alone: it was the fear of rejection.

He'd used his money to put up barriers between him and others, specifically women. He'd rejected them, saying they only wanted his money, before they could reject him. And it had worked until...

Brooke.

"Jeffrey," Matt said, putting the last piece into a puzzle, "why don't you plan on coming to our wedding tomorrow?"

"Really!"

"What?" Brooke eyes widened then narrowed. "What are you doing?"

"The only logical thing." He'd been running for too long. If he let Brooke go, he would lose the best thing that had ever come into his life.

"I won't come if you don't want me." Jeffrey rolled a puzzle piece along its edge.

"Jeffrey," Brooke said in a calmer tone, "I would love for you to come to our wedding. But…"

"Sure, I understand."

"No, you don't." She exhaled, as if feeling a heavy burden, and glared at Matt. "Why don't you explain it to him?"

"Explain what?" He knew he was provoking her anger, but he couldn't stop himself.

"Jeffrey," she asked, "would you mind giving Matt and me a few minutes alone?"

"Are you gonna fight?"

"Fight?" she repeated, giving Matt a look that said she was going to pulverize him. "There's nothing for you to worry about, Jeffrey. Everything is fine."

"It's okay, Jeffrey." Matt realized he'd pushed Brooke too far. He didn't want to alienate her. He wanted to ask her to marry him. But, dammit, how? He glanced at his watch. "It is getting late. And Dr. Watson needs her beauty rest. She has a big day tomorrow and wants to look her best for our wedding."

"Matt—"

"You are going to marry me, aren't you?" Okay, he admitted, it was a backhanded proposal. But he wasn't prepared. He'd never proposed before to a woman, especially to someone like Brooke. To someone he loved. And if she said no…

"What are you talking about?"

"Your wedding tomorrow," Jeffrey stated as if she hadn't understood the question. "Matt wants to make sure you're gonna be there. You are, aren't you, Dr. Watson?"

A strange glint in her eyes gave Matt a glimpse into her soul. Her very troubled soul. He read the confusion, the chaotic emotions churning in her depths. He wished he could make this easy for her. But it wasn't an easy decision. And he knew she didn't *want* marriage. Maybe not even him.

But he had to take the chance, he had to risk his heart or face being alone the rest of his life.

He realized in that moment that Brooke had shown him the beauty of true giving. She demonstrated through her actions how he'd kept his heart guarded, fearful of being abandoned. But no more. Not this time.

She'd given her life to these kids, to helping others. What had he done? Created an empire. But money wasn't the legacy he wanted. One day his heritage would be his family, not how many stores he'd opened or gold he'd collected. And his family had to start with Brooke, with convincing her that he loved her.

Because he realized she could give love, but she was afraid to receive it. She, too, was afraid of rejection. So now it was his turn. It was time for him to put his heart on the line for the woman he loved and take the biggest risk of his life.

Jeffrey yawned, his jaws widening until they creaked, and stretched his arms wide. "I am kinda tired."

"Why don't you go on to bed," Matt suggested. "Tomorrow's going to be busy. I'll pick you up about ten in the morning. Then you can help me get ready. Okay?''

"Matt?'' Brooke touched his arm. "We really need to talk about this.''

"What's there to talk about?'' Matt asked, covering her hand with his.

Jeffrey hopped up from the table. "See ya.''

"Night, Jeffrey,'' Matt said. "Hey!''

The little boy turned back to face them.

"You're not planning on running off between now and tomorrow morning, are you?''

"Nope.''

"Promise?''

He nodded. "Sorry that I scared y'all. I won't do it again.''

"Good,'' Brooke said. "Just remember you can always talk to one of us.''

After the little boy had left the rec room and headed toward his room, Brooke turned on Matt. "What was that all about? How are you going to explain to him tomorrow that there isn't going to be a wedding?''

"I won't have to.''

She crossed her arms over her chest. "What do you mean?''

"Because there is going to be a wedding. That is, if you'll agree to marry me.''

Chapter Twelve

"Have you lost your mind?" Brooke asked. She stared at Matt as if his hair had just turned purple. That wouldn't have surprised her any more than his sudden off-the-cuff marriage proposal.

It was a proposal, wasn't it? A real proposal this time. Or had she imagined it? Her heart skittered to a halt, then raced as if she was running out of breath, running out of time.

"Did you ask me to marry you?" She watched him closely for signs that he'd gone over the edge. Or maybe she had. "As in *really* marry you? The till-death-do-us-part kind? Like becoming husband and wife, forever and ever? Not to make your grandmother happy? Not to get my matchmaking mother off my back? But because—"

"Yes." He pushed away from the miniature table and clasped her hands. "Do you want me to get down on my knees?"

Stunned, she could only shake her head.

What was he doing? He was ruining everything! It wasn't supposed to turn out this way. They were supposed to break up, part ways, say goodbye. Adios. *Hasta la vista,* baby. What had happened to her neat and tidy plan? To her heart?

Matt. The answer was simple. *He* had changed everything. Including the rules they'd set up.

Now she could only stare at him, afraid to move forward, but more terrified to run away.

"Look," he said, "I may not have said it right. I may not have done it right. But I'm not up on the proper etiquette for proposing to my make-believe fiancée." The lines around his mouth deepened. The different glints of color in his eyes, like a swirling display of churning clouds and midnight mist, reflected the tumultuous emotions churning inside her. "But the truth is I love you."

Love. Did he really know what it meant? That it was a verb, not a whimsical emotion that could later be tossed aside, along with her?

"You love me?" she repeated dully, but her heart banged against her breast bone.

"Do you…could you love me?"

"I…I don't know." She felt herself trembling, and she crossed her arms over her chest to try to hold herself together before she came unraveled.

Why couldn't she say she loved him? Why couldn't she get the words past the lump in her throat? Was she like her mother? Waiting for someone else, someone better to come along? Who could be a better catch than Matt Cutter?

Say it, Brooke! Tell him. Before it's too late.

"At least you're honest." Something in his eyes dimmed. Then he turned away.

Suddenly she felt cold, a shiver rippling through her, making her limbs numb. "Matt—"

"It's okay. At one time I would have thought I was foolish for even suggesting such a thing or admitting my love. But not now. I guess I've learned that love doesn't demand anything in return. Even if you don't love me, I still love you. That won't change."

"This is all so sudden," she said. "I'm so confused."

"I know. Me, too. Or I was. But now I see everything clearly." His shoulders looked stiff. "Maybe I threw this at you too suddenly. Maybe you need time.

"I'll be there tomorrow. At the mission. For our wedding." He jammed his hands in his front pockets. "Waiting at the front." His gaze met hers, hot, heavy, demanding. "Waiting for you."

Then he turned and left her alone with doubts, confusion and pain caving in on her.

"You're not dressed yet," Felicia observed, as she barreled into Brooke's entryway, her gaze skimming over the mismatched sweats Brooke had put on late the night before. She set down a champagne bottle, her mother-of-the-bride designer dress and a makeup bag. "I decided to have a manicure. What do you think?" She waggled her fingers. "Pink Passion."

"It's pink all right."

"And I brought champagne. Your wedding is definitely something to celebrate. I thought we should start early."

Brooke closed the door to her apartment and sat at her dining room table. She took a long slow gulp of coffee. She'd been sitting in the same spot all night, feeling too tired to move, too exhausted to search for the answer to her dilemma.

"What's wrong?" Her mother's brow folded into worry lines. "Has something happened?"

"Yeah, I guess you could say that."

"Oh, dear." Felicia sank like a deflated balloon into the chair opposite Brooke. "Did you chase Matt away? Did he break up with you?"

"Not exactly. He wants to marry me!"

Felicia blinked. "And the problem is…?"

With a heavy sigh, Brooke confessed their charade, giving her the highlights of the plan Matt and she had agreed to at the beginning. "But he changed the rules."

"Doesn't seem to be much of a problem to me. This is good." Her face relaxed, obviously relieved she hadn't lost a dream son-in-law.

"How do you know that?" she asked, sounding defensive even to herself.

"It's obvious you love him. And he loves you."

"Why do you say that?"

"Because you so often point out I'm an expert on marriage…what works and what doesn't. And your marriage to Matt is going to work out just fine."

"But, Mother…" She sighed and slid her fingers through her hair. "I don't know. I'm not sure."

"Sure, you are. If you didn't love him, wouldn't you be wondering how you were going to let him down gently?"

"Maybe. Maybe not. I do care for him."

Felicia rolled her eyes. "Oh, please! I've seen the way you look at him. And the way he looks at you. Why, you two make it hot enough to declare a national emergency."

So the sparks hadn't been imagined. Or maybe others had wanted to see sparks between them. Or maybe Brooke had wanted sparks. Maybe there was something…or someone significant missing from her life. But was it Matt?

Quit denying the fact that you love him! What's wrong with you? She didn't know the answer. But fear immobilized her.

"What is it you're afraid of losing?" her mother asked. "Your independence? Your home? Your freedom?"

My heart.

Brooke clasped her hands around her coffee mug as if seeking comfort or warmth from the chill permeating her body. "But—"

"What? Are you such a stickler for the rules that you can't change course midstream?"

"Maybe."

"Let me ask you a question. Are you scared you're going to be like me?"

"No, I'm scared Matt's going to be like you. What if *he* gets tired of me? What if this is just a passing fancy? I mean, he's known for going through women like most people plow through a bag of potato chips."

Felicia placed her hand over Brooke's. "Do you really believe that about him? Or is this just an excuse?"

"What do you mean?"

"I don't think the issue is me at all." A strength and wisdom shone in her mother's eyes. "I think it's your father."

Brooke crossed her arms over her chest. "You don't know what you're talking about."

"Just because you have a psychology degree doesn't mean you're smarter than the rest of us."

She lifted her brows in surprise. "Go ahead."

"Your father..." Felicia softened her voice and approach "...was never good at saying 'I love you.' And unfortunately, I think you're the same way."

Her spine bristled. "I can say...it."

"When?"

"Every day. What do you think I do at the orphanage three days a week? I care deeply about my patients. If I didn't care, I wouldn't try to help them like I do."

"Okay, you're a good psychologist. But that doesn't make you a good lover."

"Excuse me?"

"A good lover can say I love you. You can't. Or you never do. You assume this analytical, clinical mind-set, and you don't let anyone get too close. Even me. Because you're afraid of getting hurt."

"So, Ms. Psychology, why do you think I do that?"

"Because of your father."

"Mother, he's distant because of you. Because he's afraid of being hurt. Remember, you left him. You saw greener pastures and dumped him for someone who made more money."

"That's not true."

"Oh, Mother. Please. I have eyes. I know what happened."

"You think you know what happened. I loved your father. Deeply. But he couldn't return my love. He couldn't say 'I love you.' Even before I left him. And that's one reason I left him. Another reason I left was that he'd found someone else."

"What? You never told me that."

"Because I didn't want to prejudice you against your father or men. It happens. He was away from home a lot. A distance grew between us. He left emotionally a long time before I packed my bags."

Her mother's explanation struck her like a palm to her face. Could it be possible? Did it really matter? The fact was, she had put up walls around her heart to protect herself from being hurt. "Why didn't you ever tell me?"

"If I'd understood your warped perception of what happened then maybe I would have. You were too young at the time to understand."

It's something Brooke had never considered. She knew then she wasn't worried about Matt racing off to another woman. He wasn't like her mother or her father. He wasn't afraid to commit, hoping someone better would come along. She knew that in the depth of her heart and soul. After all, she'd seen the way he cared for his grandmother, loved her, bent over backward to make her happy.

"But my marriage to your father…and my marriages since are not the issue at hand. What are you going to do about Matt?" Felicia asked.

"I don't know. I have to think about it," she hedged.

"Well, don't take too long analyzing the situation, Brooke. Otherwise you might just miss the best opportunity of your life."

"What was that all about?" Eliza Cutter crossed her arms over her chest.

Matt snapped his cellular phone closed and clapped

Jeffrey on the shoulder. He'd asked the boy to be his best man today. "Nothing. Everything is okay."

"Don't you have anything better to do at this moment than work? You are so like your grandfather." His grandmother's complexion turned pink with irritation. It was the first time since his grandfather's death that she'd said anything negative about him. It was a good sign. She was being realistic with her memories.

"Why doesn't that sound like a compliment?"

"Because there is more to life than work. Your grandfather didn't know that until it was too late. But I know it. And I want you to know it, too. There are guests waiting out there. For goodness' sake! You're about to get married."

"That phone call didn't have anything to do with work." He paced along the stone floor. Glancing at his watch, he saw it was time.

"Sounded like work, what with all that legalese you were spouting."

"I was speaking with the attorneys at work about a private matter."

"Matthew Lincoln Cutter!" She placed her hands on her hips. "You better not be thinking about a prenuptial agreement."

"It's too late for that, Grandmother. And don't worry, I'm not." He peered through the window. The small group of family and friends gathered were sitting in the wooden pews waiting. As he was. Waiting. Waiting to see if Brooke would arrive. If she'd marry him. "Is she here yet?"

"No." She patted his arm. "But don't you worry. She's coming. I'm sure she's been delayed in traffic. I should have insisted she take the limo."

"Brooke doesn't like limos." A faint smile played about his lips as he remembered so many things about her. His heart felt weak as it pounded out each second that she didn't arrive.

What if she didn't love him? It was the first time that possibility had occurred to him. He'd blocked any other possibility out of his head. Until now. Until the guests had arrived and were waiting...waiting for both of them.

"Grandmother, I think there's something you should know about—"

"Nonsense. I don't care if you two had a tiff last night. I can spot love at twenty paces. I know you love Brooke. And it's obvious she loves you."

"It is?" His hope soared.

Eliza nodded. "Now, I'm going to go take my seat. I'd say don't worry, but I know all bridegrooms worry."

He gave her a kiss on the cheek, his heart aching as he watched her make her way to the front of the chapel and settle into the pew.

"Don't worry," Jeffrey said, reaching up and grasping Matt's hand. "Dr. Watson is gonna show."

"I hope you're right, cowboy. I really do."

"She's here!"

The announcement from the minister brought a flurry of activity. The organist began to play. Before Matt could catch a glimpse of his bride and ask her if she loved him or not, he was ushered into the chapel to take his place at the front and wait for his bride to walk down the aisle.

Alone, she moved slowly, gracefully, her steps matching the rhythm of the organ, as she made her way down the aisle toward him. Her face was veiled by gauzy fabric, but he knew she was staring straight at him.

Anxiety pumped through his veins. What was she thinking? He couldn't read her expression because of the damn veil. Why was she here? To please her mother? To finish off their charade with a tabloid type ending with somebody giving a ludicrous reason why they shouldn't get married? Or was she here because she loved him?

The whole ceremony became surreal. Matt went through the motions they'd rehearsed, taking her hand, settling it into the crook of his arm, bowing his head for a brief prayer. Out of the corner of his eye he watched Brooke, glimpsing the rosy hue of her lips, the sharp slant of her cheekbone, her calm, serene expression. What did it mean? What did she want? Him? Or peace from her matchmaking mother?

She turned toward him slightly and gave his arm a squeeze. Her hand had felt cool to his touch, but her fingers were steady. What was she saying? Goodbye? Or that she loved him?

Matt heard the beating of his own heart more than the minister as he delivered a short sermon on the purpose of marriage. He couldn't concentrate. His thoughts spun, spiraling down into the same question. Was this a pretend ceremony? Or were they really and truly getting married? Forever and ever?

"Do you, Matthew Cutter, take this woman to be your lawfully wedded wife? To have and to hold, from this day forward?" the minister asked.

Releasing her arm, he faced Brooke and took both of her hands in his. He knew without a doubt that he loved her. And he would prove it by saying *I do* first. "Yes. I do."

He watched for a sign, for any response, but she only blinked slowly as if absorbing the consequences of what he'd done.

The minister looked toward Brooke. "And do you, Brooke Watson, take this man to be your lawfully wedded husband? To have and to hold, from this day forward?"

Fear gripped him. His stomach contracted. What if she said no? What if she stepped away? What if she walked out of his life?

He couldn't let that happen.

"Wait," Matt said. He reached toward her and lifted her veil. The tears glimmering in her eyes stunned him. His heart tripped over itself. This was it. For better or worse. He prayed it wasn't the latter, prayed that she wasn't about to tell him she didn't love him. If she severed their relationship, their fake engagement, then it would shatter his heart.

"I love you," he whispered. "Doesn't that mean anything to you?"

"Yes." A teardrop glistened in the corner of her eye.

He grasped her elbows. "Then tell me. Do you love me? Will you marry me?"

"Yes."

That simple yet beautiful word rocked through him. Not believing his ears, he searched her face. Their eyes met, and a shudder of pure delight rolled over him. His gaze slipped to her mouth as it curved in a delicious smile. And he kissed her.

His arms went around her, holding her to him, and hers went around his neck. She pressed herself close to him until he felt the flutter of her heart against the pounding of his own.

"Wait a minute!" the minister said, putting a hand on Matt's shoulder. "Not yet. You're not supposed to kiss her yet. She hasn't said 'I do.'"

Forcing himself to pull away from Brooke, he gazed down at her.

"I do," she whispered.

Then he kissed her again.

"Wait!" the minister protested again.

"What?" Matt asked, still holding Brooke close.

"I'm supposed to tell you to kiss your bride."

Smiling down at his bride, his wife, absorbing the love shining in her eyes like the sun's rays, he said, "Too late."

This time Brooke rose up on her toes and pressed her mouth to his. Feeling his warmth and strength seeping into her, she knew without a doubt that she'd made the right decision. This was where she belonged—right in Matt's arms.

The minister cleared his throat. "Well, you're not married until I pronounce it."

Matt's gaze locked with Brooke's.

"By the power vested in me by the state of Texas, I pronounce you man and wife. May I present—"

"You're supposed to say I can kiss my bride now." Matt grinned.

Laughter rippled through the congregation.

"You've already done that," the minister said. "Now may I present Mr. and Mrs. Matthew Cutter."

"Do you have a problem taking my name?" Matt asked.

"Not at all." She kissed him again. "I'm proud to be Mrs. Matthew Cutter."

"Good." Still keeping one arm around her waist, he faced the congregation with his bride by his side. "But I have an announcement to make."

"That's not what we rehearsed," the minister said.

"We're more than Mr. and Mrs.," he said, lifting his voice so that everyone could hear. "We're a family." He hooked his other arm around Jeffrey's shoulders and pulled the boy close to his side. "We're adopting this boy. If he'll have us as parents."

"Cool," Jeffrey said with a wide grin.

"Thank you," Brooke whispered to Matt.

"Thank you for being my wife."

With her heart overflowing, Brooke pulled them together into a tight circle of love.

*   *   *   *   *

You're not going to believe this offer!

**In October and November 2000, buy any two Harlequin
or Silhouette books and save $10.00 off future purchases,
or buy any three and save $20.00 off future purchases!**

Just fill out this form and attach 2 proofs of purchase (cash register
receipts) from October and November 2000 books and Harlequin will
send you a coupon booklet worth a total savings of $10.00 off future
purchases of Harlequin and Silhouette books in 2001. Send us 3 proofs
of purchase and we will send you a coupon booklet worth a total
savings of $20.00 off future purchases.

Saving money has never been this easy.

I accept your offer! Please send me a coupon booklet:

Name: _____

Address: _____ City: _____

State/Prov.: _____ Zip/Postal Code: _____

Optional Survey!

In a typical month, how many Harlequin or Silhouette books would you buy <u>new</u> at retail stores?

☐ Less than 1   ☐ 1   ☐ 2   ☐ 3 to 4   ☐ 5+

Which of the following statements best describes how you <u>buy</u> Harlequin or Silhouette books?
Choose one answer only that <u>best</u> describes you.

☐ I am a regular buyer and reader
☐ I am a regular reader but buy only occasionally
☐ I only buy and read for specific times of the year, e.g. vacations
☐ I subscribe through Reader Service but also buy at retail stores
☐ I mainly borrow and buy only occasionally
☐ I am an occasional buyer and reader

Which of the following statements best describes how you <u>choose</u> the Harlequin and Silhouette
series books you buy <u>new</u> at retail stores? By "series," we mean books within a particular line,
such as *Harlequin PRESENTS* or *Silhouette SPECIAL EDITION*. Choose one answer only that
<u>best</u> describes you.

☐ I only buy books from my favorite series
☐ I generally buy books from my favorite series but also buy
   books from other series on occasion
☐ I buy some books from my favorite series but also buy from
   many other series regularly
☐ I buy all types of books depending on my mood and what
   I find interesting and have no favorite series

Please send this form, along with your cash register receipts as proofs of purchase, to:
In the U.S.: Harlequin Books, P.O. Box 9057, Buffalo, NY 14269
In Canada: Harlequin Books, P.O. Box 622, Fort Erie, Ontario L2A 5X3
(Allow 4-6 weeks for delivery) Offer expires December 31, 2000.   PHQ4002

Silhouette®

where love comes alive—online...

eHARLEQUIN.com

your romantic books

♥ Shop online! Visit Shop eHarlequin and discover a wide selection of new releases and classic favorites at great discounted prices.

♥ Read our daily and weekly Internet exclusive serials, and participate in our interactive novel in the reading room.

♥ Ever dreamed of being a writer? Enter your chapter for a chance to become a featured author in our Writing Round Robin novel.

• • • • • •

your romantic life

♥ Check out our feature articles on dating, flirting and other important romance topics and get your daily love dose with tips on how to keep the romance alive every day.

• • • • • • •

your community

♥ Have a Heart-to-Heart with other members about the latest books and meet your favorite authors.

♥ Discuss your romantic dilemma in the Tales from the Heart message board.

your romantic escapes

♥ Learn what the stars have in store for you with our daily Passionscopes and weekly Erotiscopes.

♥ Get the latest scoop on your favorite royals in Royal Romance.